T0110626

Praise for Joe R. Lansdale and

Devil Red

"If you've read more than a few words strung together by Lansdale in any given context, you're going to pick up a book with his name on the cover. . . . A new installment in the [Hap and Leonard] series is cause to rejoice."

—*Bookreporter*

"There's enough seriousness to make this novel stand far apart from run-of-the-mill thrillers— and enough comedy to have readers laughing through the blood spatters." —*Publishers Weekly*

"Lansdale is a terrifically gifted storyteller with a sharp country boy wit."

—*The Washington Post Book World*

"Hap and Leonard represent the bluest of blue-collar detective fiction." —*San Jose Mercury News*

"Joe Lansdale is one of the greatest yarn spinners of his generation: fearless, earthy, original, manic and dreadfully funny."

—*The Dallas Morning News*

Joe R. Lansdale
Devil Red

Joe R. Lansdale is the author of more than a dozen novels, including *Vanilla Ride*, *Leather Maiden*, *Sunset and Sawdust*, and *Lost Echoes*. He has received the British Fantasy Award, the American Mystery Award, the Edgar Award, the Grinzane Cavour Prize for Literature, and seven Bram Stoker Awards. He lives with his family in Nacogdoches, Texas.

www.joerlansdale.com

Also by Joe R. Lansdale

In the Hap and Leonard Series

Vanilla Ride
Captains Outrageous
Rumble Tumble
Bad Chili
The Two-Bear Mambo
Mucho Mojo
Savage Season

Other Novels

Leather Maiden
Lost Echoes
Sunset and Sawdust
The Bottoms
A Fine Dark Line
Freezer Burn

Devil Red

Devil Red

JOE R. LANSDALE

VINTAGE CRIME/BLACK LIZARD

Vintage Books

A Division of Random House, Inc.

New York

FIRST VINTAGE CRIME/BLACK LIZARD EDITION, MARCH 2012

The Library of Congress has cataloged the Knopf edition as follows:
Lansdale, Joe R.
Devil red / Joe R. Lansdale.
p. cm.
1. Collins, Hap (Fictitious character)—Fiction. 2. Pine, Leonard (Fictitious
character)—Fiction. 3. Assassins—Fiction.
4. Inheritance and succession—Fiction. 5. Cults—Fiction. 6. Texas—Fiction.
I. Title.
PS3562.A557D48 2011
813'.54—dc22
2010047476

Vintage ISBN: 978-0-307-45546-8

Book design by Virginia Tan

www.vintagebooks.com

This one's for Karen

You are what you do.

—*Old proverb*

if I bet on Humanity
I'd never cash a ticket.

—*Charles Bukowski*

Devil Red

1

We were parked at the curb in Leonard's car, sitting near a busted-out streetlight. We were looking at a house about a block up. It was a dark house on a dark street next to another dark house, and beyond that was an abandoned baseball field grown up with summer-burnt grass that had died two months back but was still standing, the tops curved over like bent sword tips. A fresh fall wind was bullying some dead leaves about and we had the windows rolled down and the air was cool and soothing. Beyond the baseball field it was dark too.

The whole area wasn't exactly what you'd call a great place to hang out. You did, there was a chance they'd find you next morning in a ditch with your throat cut, your pockets turned inside out, and sperm in your ass, or perhaps a sharp instrument. It was the kind of place where the mice belonged to gangs.

But there we sat. Sacrifices to fate.

I said, "I feel like a hired leg breaker."

"You are a hired leg breaker," Leonard said.

"This is pretty mean."

"He beat up an old woman, Hap. Took her money. That's so mean the mean has to wear a hat and tie."

"A hat and tie?"

"It's an expression."

"No it's not."

"All right. I made it up."

"Of course you did."

"Thing is," Leonard said, "the cops didn't do dick."

"They took him in for questioning."

"Whoop-te-doo," Leonard said. "And it was Mrs. Johnson's word against his and now he's free and he's sleeping in that house, him and his bud, and they got the old lady's money."

"The bud didn't hit her," I said.

"Yeah, well, the bud ought not to hang around with the wrong people."

"I hang around with you."

"But I'm charmin'," Leonard said, cracking his knuckles. "You ready?"

"I don't know," I said.

"What's to think about? We took the job."

"The money for one. Twenty-five dollars, to split. Really? That's our payment?"

"Since when do you worry about money?"

"Since it's twelve fifty."

"It'll pay us back for those cheap-ass baseball bats," Leonard said.

"It will at that. We might even make a quarter or two when it's all over."

"So what are you complainin' about? You're comin' out ahead."

"We could go to jail. That's one complaint. It could be me and you and Marvin and Mrs. Johnson, all of us sitting on a cot in a jail cell knitting sweaters with the words DUMB ASS across the front."

Leonard sighed, leaned back in his seat, and adopted a tone akin to a father about to explain to a son why making bad grades in high school won't get you far in life. "This douche bag ain't gonna say squat. He's got a badass reputation to maintain. Think he wants to say he got caught off guard and beat up by a worn-out honky and a handsome majestic queer with baseball bats?"

"Reputation? He beat up an old lady, what kind of reputation is that?"

"He probably doesn't advertise that part, just the stuff about him being a big gangster and all. He's a legend in his own mind. We're just here to get Mrs. Johnson's money back."

"We're going to rough somebody up for eighty-eight dollars?"

"And some change."

"Yeah, don't want to forget that, Leonard. He got another forty-five cents."

"Forty-six. If you're living on a fixed income, it matters. And, hey, we're getting twenty-five dollars of it, and Marvin, he's got a cut comin'."

"You know we won't take any of it, and he won't either, and that this isn't a real job. This is a favor. Marvin to her, us to him."

"Yeah, but we can pretend," Leonard said. "It's fun. Didn't you ever play pretend?"

I gave Leonard a sour look. "While we're pretending, guys in the house might be serious. And I'm tired of beating up people and getting beat up."

"All right, then. I'll do the hitting. You don't break anything. Him or the furniture. We'll just let him know we don't like him doin' what he's been doin', and I'll hit him on the meaty parts."

"You're just saying that, aren't you? You're going to break something."

Leonard was silent for a time. "He broke her hand, so I got to think maybe his hand has to get broken. But you don't have to do dick in that department, brother. Just come and watch out for his friend. The big guy, Chunk. I might not want him runnin' up my ass."

"Isn't the friend's supposed to be pretty damn big," I said.

"Would it put you in better spirits if you broke the guy's hand and I watched for the big guy?"

"No."

"Hell, man. You get to choose. Which is it?"

I sighed. "You do the breaking."

"So we're on?"

"Yeah, but remember, when we're doing a stretch at Huntsville, I didn't like the idea."

"Noted," Leonard said. "I'll even give you my bread in the prison cafeteria."

"What's this guy's name again?"

"What's it matter?"

"I like to know who I'm beating up."

"Thomas Traney took the money. The big guy, he's called Chunk, that's all I know. You heard this already."

"Yeah, but I wasn't listening so good. I didn't think we were really going to do it. Next we'll be twisting grade-schooler's wrists to find out who took whose lunch money. Or maybe we can take their lunch money ourselves, being tough guys and all."

"You through bitchin'?" Leonard said, pulling on a pair of skin-tight gloves, then handing me a pair.

I nodded, put on the gloves, leaned over the seat and got the baseball bats, and handed one to Leonard.

2

We got out of the car and started across the dark yard, went over the dry grass, and up on the back porch. I looked back toward the baseball field and the dark there, just in case someone was watching.

Nothing.

Leonard leaned an ear against the door.

"Quieter than a politician's brain," Leonard said.

"We ought to leave it that way."

Leonard touched the door and pushed gently. "This is a weak and shitty door," he said.

I didn't say anything this time. I knew it was too late. It was on.

Leonard stepped back and stomp-kicked the door hard. The door's lock broke and there was a sound of splintered wood and the door swung wide and slammed against the wall, and we were in.

There was a hallway, and we went along that quick. There was a room to the left with the door open, and I looked in there. There was nothing but heaps of trash. I looked at Leonard and shook my head. The house stank of cigarettes.

Leonard went down the hall ahead of me, a man on a mission. I rushed to keep up. He boldly opened a door on the right and went in and I looked in after him. There was a mattress on the floor, and a woman on it, and there was a window to her right and a bit of moonlight coming through it. All I could tell about her was she was dark-skinned and her eyes were wide and she was nude from the waist up; the rest of her was covered in bedclothes. I knew from the way her head went a little to my left that she was watching someone in the corner, and I said, "Watch it!"

Leonard wheeled and a gun fired and everything went bright for a moment and a bullet whistled through the air and smacked into the wall. I saw Leonard move, and he was across the room fast as an arrow in flight. I could hear the air split as he swung the bat. The gun barked again from the shadows, and I jumped. I rushed inside the room, even though I wanted to do anything but that.

Leonard had someone on the floor in the corner and his bat went up and then down. The person on the floor screamed, and I heard something behind me. I turned in time to see a black giant in undershorts fill the doorway, then come into the room carrying a cane knife, wearing a moonlit expression that wouldn't pass for humor.

He cocked back the cane knife and I swung the bat at him, hit him in the shin. He barked and stumbled. I hit him again, this time in the side. I heard him grunt and he dropped the cane knife at my feet. I put one foot on it and pushed it back and away from me, into the shadows.

I heard Leonard's bat come down hard, and I heard him say, "How do you like it?"

But I had my own business. The giant tried to get up and I hit him across his broad back. He made with another grunt but got up, and I swung for his kneecap. He went down screaming, rolling on the floor, clutching at his knee. His shadow rolled and crawled along the wall with him.

Leonard said to his man, "You got some money?"

The guy on the floor, who I figured was Thomas, was only wearing undershorts. Just as a fashion note, his and Chunk's shorts did not match. He said, "You robbin' me?"

"Nope," Leonard said. "I'm takin' back somethin' you took that don't belong to you. Where's your wallet? And you better hope there's money in it."

Thomas had one hand up, to try and ward off the bat. He was otherwise stretched out on the floor, his head lifted a little.

"My pants are on the floor, by the bed. Wallet's in the back pocket."

"I'm on it," I said. I went over and found his pants and took out his wallet and went over to the window where the moonlight was shining in. I stood to the side so I could watch the big man on the floor. He was still rolling around moaning and clutching at his knee. I figured I had destroyed it. It had been one hell of a swing.

"He's got maybe three hundred dollars," I said.

"Take a hundred," Leonard said, standing over his victim, the bat raised. "That covers what's owed, plus a bit for our time and him trying to shoot us, and a little extra for the bats."

I took out the hundred and dropped the wallet on the floor. I looked at the girl. She was kind of pretty, or would be with twenty pounds on her. The last meal she looked to have had probably came out of a needle and didn't have taste. I wanted to save her, of course. I wanted to save everyone. I wanted to be somewhere else as well, and I wanted to be someone else, and I wished I hadn't flunked algebra in high school.

I held up the hundred. "Got it," I said.

"Good," Leonard said.

"You're crazy, man," said Thomas. "I'll come for you."

"I don't think so," Leonard said. "You're a fuckin' coward."

I saw the man turn his head and look at the gun he had fired. It was on the floor where Leonard had disarmed it. It was maybe six feet away.

Leonard said, "That's right, go for it. I'd love to make a homer with your head." Leonard lightly tapped Thomas's shoulder with the ball bat.

I could see by the way Thomas's shoulders drooped that hope for the gun had gone the way of his young dreams. He was screwed and he knew it.

"Let me leave you with two bits of advice, one verbal, the other demonstrative," Leonard said. "First, don't rob and hurt old ladies. Second," and with that Leonard brought the bat down on Thomas's hand where it rested on the floor. The scream Thomas let out crawled up my back and nestled at the top of my skull and took a shit.

"That's the demonstrative tip," Leonard said. "That's to let you know messin' with and hurtin' an old lady, that's gonna get you hurt. You come back, you touch her, next time they find you it'll be with this bat up your ass and your dead mouth wrapped around Chunk's dead dick."

Thomas was holding his hand, which, in the moonlight, looked kind of flat to me. He was breathing fast and lying on the floor, completely stretched out. A sound like a dying mouse seeped out of his mouth.

Leonard leaned over him. "Let me make it even more clear. You bother me, or send someone to bother me, or my brother here, provided you even know who I am, who he is, and I'll kill them, and then I'll kill you, even if I don't know for sure you sent them. And then I'll kill you after your dead. That's how much I'll kill you. Savvy, asshole?"

Thomas had his mouth open and was holding his hand. It was like he wanted to speak but nothing would come out.

"Savvy!" Leonard said.

"Savvy," Thomas said.

"That's good." Leonard said, then went over and picked up the gun and put it in his belt. He looked back at Thomas. "I'm not just whistlin' out of my ass. I mean what I say."

"Yeah," said Thomas. "I got you."

"But do you believe me?"

"I do."

"Let me hear an amen."

Thomas looked at Leonard like he'd lost his mind. So did I. Leonard just kept looking at Thomas, waiting.

"Amen," Thomas finally said.

"That's right, ass wipe," Leonard said, turned toward the door, stopped, and looked down at the giant. He said, "You can get big as you want, Chunk, but eyes and balls and kneecaps, they're what we like to call vulnerable. Tell him, Hap."

"Vulnerable," I said.

"Don't let me see your ass around either," Leonard said. "You might consider a different climate. Comprehend what I'm saying?"

The man didn't speak. Everyone in the room was so quiet, we could hear their IQs drop. Of course, they didn't have far to fall.

Leonard kicked him on the kneecap he was holding. Chunk bellowed.

"Well," Leonard said.

"I understand," Chunk said.

I looked down at Chunk, and even in the dark, I could tell he was looking at Leonard the way I sometimes looked at him, like he was looking into a deep dark pit that had no bottom.

"Good," Leonard said. "Our work here is done."

I looked at the woman on the bed, said, "Probably goes without sayin', but maybe you might not want to say or do anything either. And you're maybe two pounds shy of organ failure. Eat something greasy."

She nodded.

"Good," I said. "Thanks."

3

Out back we slung the baseball bats in the direction of the ball field. We went and got in the car. Leonard said, "You thanked her? And gave her a diet tip?"

"It just sort of came out," I said.

"It took the edge off my witty remarks."

"Sorry."

"Well," Leonard said. "You got to be you. How about we go by Wal-Mart, buy some cookies-and-cream ice cream, some vanilla wafers to dip in it?"

"Nothing like leg breaking and desert," I said.

"I broke the motherfucker's hand, and I think I got a rib too," Leonard said. "You're the one broke a leg. A kneecap."

"I can still hear it crack," I said.

"Maybe we'll get a couple cartons of ice cream, brother."

Leonard started up his car and pulled out.

I said, "That really made you feel good, didn't it, Leonard? Hittin' that guy."

"I don't know good is how I feel, but satisfied sort of fits," Leonard said. "And he didn't shoot me, so I feel good about that. Motherfucker would have done better to throw the gun at me, his aim was so bad."

Leonard took Thomas's gun out of his waistband and handed it to me and I popped out the clip and cleaned it with a Kleenex. I wrapped the clip in the Kleenex and Leonard drove by a Dumpster behind a mall and I dropped it in. Then we drove out to the edge of town and I wiped the pistol clean and wrapped it in a piece of newspaper from the backseat and gave it to Leonard and he carried it out into the woods. When he came back, he said, "There now, all done. I dropped it down an armadillo hole."

"If we hear of armadillos taking over possum kingdom, then we know what happened," I said.

We took off our gloves, Leonard drove us to Wal-Mart, and we bought ice cream and cookies. I didn't say much when we got to Leonard's place, which was recently rented and cheap and in a part of town only slightly better than the one we had just left. We went upstairs and sat in fold-out chairs in a corner that served as a kitchen at a crate that served as a table, and with a spoon apiece, and cookies to dip, we ate and counted roaches racing across the floor. There were a lot of roaches, and some of them were bigger than my thumb. I was glad Brett wasn't around for a change. She would charge a rhino if she felt it necessary, but the clicking of roach legs on linoleum could run her ten miles and make her climb a tree.

When we were done eating, Leonard said, "You want to go home, or you gonna stay?"

"Drive me home," I said. "Brett will be waiting. Besides, I don't want to get eaten by roaches."

"You have gotten so persnickety," Leonard said. "I remember a time when you would have named them, made them each little hats, and called them your friends."

4

On the drive to my place, Leonard shifted his eyes over to me and sighed. He said, "You're sitting there all forlorn."

"I feel forlorn," I said.

"Some things you do, not because they're pleasant, but because they have to be done."

"But I'm not sure that was one of them."

"You got way too many feelings, Hap."

"I suppose."

"Look at it this way, brother. I got feelings too, but they're for those who deserve feelings. There are some people don't have feelings, and don't deserve yours. The only kind of feelings they got are pain and fear."

"Governments use that tactic. Never seems to work too well."

"We ain't governments," Leonard said, as he pulled into my drive. I got out and walked around on his side and looked at him through his open window. He said, "I'll see you tomorrow at Marvin's."

I nodded. He looked at me for a while longer, almost said something, but didn't. He backed the car into the street and I watched him drive away.

I went inside and locked up and went as quietly as I could upstairs and into the bedroom. I could see Brett's shape in the bed. I took off my clothes and pulled on my pajama bottoms and got in bed as carefully as possible. When I was positioned, Brett said, "What you been doin'?"

"Killing what's left of my soul, baby."

Brett rolled over and put her arm across my chest. She smelled good. "You got the old woman's money back, didn't you?"

"We did."

"I figured you were gonna do that."

"Last thing I said when I went out was I wasn't gonna do it. I told myself that when I met up with Leonard. Told myself that when we parked out front of the house where those guys were, and I told myself that up until the moment I swung the baseball bat and took out a kneecap."

"I knew you were gonna do it."

"But what is it about me that made you know that? What's wrong with me?"

"You think things ought to be fair, and they aren't, and you try and make them fair."

"I broke a guy's kneecap. Leonard, he broke the other guy's hand and maybe a rib, and we scared a young woman who was there. I don't know how fair that was. We were so mean our mean wore a hat and tie."

"What?"

"Nothing."

Brett rubbed my chest a little, said, "Was he a good guy? Guy's knee you broke?"

"Not in the least."

"Did you hurt the girl that was there?"

"No reason to . . . No. Of course not."

"Okay. Guy's hand that Leonard broke. Was he a good guy?"

I knew where this was going, but I went ahead with the ritual. "He's the guy broke the old lady's hand, took her money."

"There you go. If he's the bad guy, you got to be the good guy."

"Who says?"

"Me. I just did."

"Yeah, well, you're sort of on my side."

"Big-time. A guy takes an old woman's money and breaks her hand and she goes to Marvin for help, what are you gonna do? She deserves her money back. It's not the first time you've helped someone and had to get rough. Hell, I've had to get rough."

"I know that. But this wasn't self-defense, and it wasn't personal."

"Anytime you can help someone get back at a bully, it's personal enough. Baby, you got to learn how to tell the good guys from the bad guys."

"You sound like Leonard."

"He can be wise when he sounds like me," Brett said. We lay there for a while. Brett stroked my chest. "I got to leave tomorrow. Early."

"Damn. I forgot."

"Figured you did. You been kind of preoccupied with your morality and your mortality . . . But it's okay. I won't be gone long. A week maybe."

"That's too long," I said.

"Poor baby. You're in the dumps."

"Big-time."

"Because you got shot a while back?"

"Well, duh, that has something to do with it," I said.

"Would some sympathy pussy help?"

"Well," I said. "I don't know I'll feel any more right about what I did, and I won't miss you any less when you're gone, but it certainly would improve my spirits."

"I thought it might," Brett said, shifting to slip off her panties.

5

I slept a short while after we made love, and then I woke up and got out of bed gently and went to the bathroom. I came back and sat in the chair by the window. I looked out at the yard where a fence rose up and another house swelled on that side slightly covered by a large tree and its shadows. The darkness from the tree made the house look like a natural formation. There was moonlight in the next-door neighbor's backyard, which was clear of trees, and there was a kid's swing set back there; it looked like some kind of Martian insect lurking.

I turned and watched Brett while she slept. The window was framed in such a way that it had four panes and the panes were filled with moonlight and the light lay across the bed and the thin slats that held the panes in place divided her like dark straight cuts. Her face was at peace and her mouth was open and she was snoring slightly. I could see her white teeth and the way her long red hair, which looked dark as the shadows, curled around her chin and spread out on the pillow like an oil spill.

I loved the way she looked and the way she made love and the way she made me feel. But there was nothing she did or could do that would make me feel good about what I had done. Not tonight, anyway.

I thought about going downstairs and reading, maybe listening to music with the earphones, but I didn't feel strongly enough about it to do it. I went back to the bathroom and closed the door and turned on the light and found a magazine on the back of the toilet, picked up the pair of Wal-Mart glasses I kept in there—I kept several pairs around the house—and put them on and sighed because I needed the damn things to read close-up print. I was too tired and too old to be beating people up. A man who was old enough for reading glasses should have a job in some place air-conditioned and his most violent activity should be sliding his zipper down.

I read from the magazine, but nothing I read stayed with me. I finally gave it up and took a couple of light sleeping pills and went back to bed, and when I woke up it was late morning and Brett was gone.

6

It hadn't been that long since I had healed up from a bullet wound, and in the process of getting that wound, I had ended up splitting some good money with Leonard, so I wasn't sure why I was working. It wasn't my style to do something when there was money already to be had. I preferred desperation and overdue bills as a work incentive.

I showered and got ready for work and thought about Brett and her whore of a daughter. Brett had gone off to see her before and had come back blue and not so friendly for a couple of days, and then she would see it all for what it was, come around, and be okay for months. Then some idea would strike her, or the daughter would e-mail her, or some such thing, and the blues would open up again like a deep hole in the sea, and down Brett would go. I couldn't do a thing for her when she was that way. She had to deal with the depths and what was down there in her own manner and in her own time, same as me. She got like that, she was nothing like she was the rest of the time, and it was really best she did leave me for a while. That way they wouldn't find my decapitated head on my pillow.

But she was never like me. She was always able to find some truth in herself. Me, I wasn't sure I knew which way was up, let alone which way was true.

As I finished getting ready, I thought too about how I had come by the money I now had in reserve. Vanilla Ride, the beautiful assassin who had been hired to kill me, gave it to me and Leonard as a gift. It had worked out strangely, with me and her and Leonard in a cabin in Arkansas. Nothing as kinky as that sounds. The three of us bonded together for a moment to have a shootout with Clete Jimson's Dixie Mafia goons. The goons didn't do well. I came out with a wound that a good veterinarian took care of. But, most important, we had parted from Vanilla with a truce intact and a pile of dough that had belonged to some un-savory characters who I liked to believe would just spend it on unsavory things. It was still hard for me to grasp the insanity of it, or to understand how someone like Vanilla could be so deadly, and yet, in her own way, honorable.

It was also hard to believe that the very man who had wanted us killed, Clete Jimson, we had also formed a truce with, primarily because we had made it not worth his while, and there was in the background the threat of Vanilla Ride, and Jimson hadn't wanted any part of that. No one in their right mind would.

I was ready just before noon and sat at the table drinking decaf-feinated coffee, waiting for Leonard to pick me up. Our friend Marvin Hanson had started a private detective agency. His plan was to hire us as grunts from time to time, which was best, because as detectives we made very good grunts.

Today we were supposed to meet him at the office to talk about a real job, not getting some old lady's money back. Then we were supposed to go to lunch and put a game plan together. What I wanted to do was go back to bed and read, or watch some TV, or just lie around on the couch. But if fish could fly they'd live in trees.

About eleven-twenty, Leonard showed up and drove us over to Marvin's office. The car had a smattering of bird crap across the windshield, and Leonard tried to clean it by turning on the wind-shield wipers, which made a slick whitish smear across the glass. Leonard cursed at it and hit the wipers again and made it worse than before.

I made a note to self. Do not try and clean bird shit off a wind-shield by using the wipers. It doesn't work. Cursing does not clean it either.

7

Marvin's office was in a nice area off the main drag, down a house-lined street. We parked in front of a huge, broad oak and got out. A space of dirt had been left in a rare example of city planning. Someone, perhaps leaving it as a kind of sacrifice to the forest gods, had placed a used rubber and a potato chip bag by the tree trunk, and it smelled like someone had taken a piss, but otherwise it looked natural and lovely and gave off a bony kind of shade.

As we sniffed the urine on the fall air, brown oak leaves were dropping and tumbling across the lot with a crackling noise, like someone stepping on paper sacks, or like someone breaking a big guy's knee with a baseball bat.

Across the way, a sweet gum tree had shed messy gum balls onto the concrete in a way that made me fear for its future with the city council.

Marvin's office was in a two-story building next to a one-story comic shop with a big blue blow-up gorilla on the roof. Some days it was a giant red ant, and on other days it was a big silver alien. One day there was a great brown bear wearing Bermuda shorts with a fish in its air-filled teeth and a fishing rod in its paw.

The bottom part of the building Marvin was in was a bike shop. The building had been painted a bright yellow. A young blonde woman, who from the shape of her legs looked like she rode a lot of bikes herself, was out front, defying the cool, wearing shorts and a T-shirt and flip-flops. She was unlocking the bike shop door when we came up. She turned and flicked her long blonde hair and smiled. She had a smile that would make a family-values Republican stab a hole in the Holy Bible with a buck knife.

The stairs were metal and a little slick from the rain that had come and gone. We went up. On the door was a sign, black letters on a green plaque. It read HANSON INVESTIGATIONS.

Inside Marvin was behind his new desk and a middle-aged woman was sitting in the client chair. She turned and looked at us as we entered. She was good-looking in a church lady, next-door-neighbor kind of way. She was dressed well, but not fancy, and her hair was a little too red and so were her cheeks. She looked as if she had been crying. She had a tissue balled up in her fist, a piece of it escaping between her fingers as if the stuffing was coming out of her. I assumed this was the client he had asked us to meet.

There was a young man with her. He was pouring coffee into a Styrofoam cup. He was tall with shaggy black hair and looked fit and had an air about him that made you think he might be tough and know it. At the same time, he looked like something for the girls. He stirred his coffee with a plastic spoon, came over, and sat in another of the client chairs. That was the end of the client chairs. That meant Leonard and I had to stand. I decided I didn't want to do that, so I went around and shoved my butt onto the edge of Marvin's desk and rested there. This put me so I was right in front of the guy. Leonard leaned against the wall, near the door, not too far from the lady. He put his hands in his pants pockets.

Marvin, who no longer needed his cane as of a month back, got up from behind his desk and limped over to the water cooler and put some water in a paper cup and brought it to the lady.

He looked at us, said, "This is Mrs. Christopher, and this is a family friend, Cason Statler. He works for the newspaper over in Camp Rapture. Folks, this is Hap Collins and this is Leonard Pine. If they say something embarrassing, understand they're friends of mine and I have to put up with it."

"Nice introduction," I said.

Mrs. Christopher smiled a little, sipped at her water.

Marvin said to us, "They're clients. They want us to check into something."

From the way the woman acted, I figured she had some romantic problems, a husband straying, or perhaps her husband had died and something was unresolved and we were supposed to resolve it. Whatever, I figured it would be simple and pretty near honest work.

"So, you'll look into it?" the lady asked.

"I will," Marvin said. "I'll put these two right on it."

"They look tough," she said.

"They are," Marvin said.

"What I mean to ask is," she said, "are they detectives?"

"They are operatives," Marvin said.

I thought: Yeah, baby. Operatives. That's us. We're so operative, our operative wears a hat and tie.

I glanced down at the desk and saw a check there in front of Marvin. It had Juanita Christopher's name signed on it. Better yet, it had a juicy figure written on it. I wondered how much of that was mine and Leonard's.

"Satisfaction guaranteed, or we give you half your money back," Marvin said. "By the way, how'd you find out about us?"

"I saw your add in Cason's newspaper."

"Just curious," Marvin said, "so I have some understanding of how my advertising works. What drew you to the ad?"

"Your last name. My maiden name was Hanson, but since you're black and I'm white, maybe there's no connection."

I thought to myself there might be a lot of connection. In this part of the country the richer branch of the Hanson family had been slave owners, so it wouldn't have surprised me to discover there were some woodshed relatives.

"Oh," Mrs. Christopher said, "I didn't mean that to sound the way it came out."

"It didn't sound any kind of way," Marvin said. "Don't worry about it."

She stood up from behind the desk and stuck her hand across at Marvin and he shook it.

She didn't sit back down, and she didn't shake our hands. "I think I've explained everything, Mr. Hanson. I'll let you fill your men in."

Hanson nodded, and she started for the door. Statler stood and spoke to her. "Do you mind if I meet you in the car, dear? I want a word with the gentlemen. You can handle the stairs fine, can't you? And watch how slick it is."

"I'm not an invalid," she said. "I'm just sad."

"Of course," Cason said, turning on a smile that if it had been an inch wider and a smidgen brighter, might have knocked out the local electric grid.

After she went out, Cason waited a moment, picked up the check she had written from the desk, and returned to his seat and rested the check on one knee with his hand on top of it. We all watched the check like buzzards discovering what was thought to be dead might still have some life in it, and just might get away.

Cason said, "I know what she told you seems like an impossible job, because of the time factor. It's a cold case. But I want to say, she's serious. I brought her over here because she's a friend of my mom's and because I know a little about her subject. I'm a newspaper reporter. I've looked into this case, there's something to it."

"So," Leonard said, "what you're saying is don't just cash her check and hang out here drinking coffee?"

"Something like that," Cason said.

Marvin said, "I not only resent that, I resent it enough to come out from behind this desk and slap the shit out of you. Even if one of these boys has to hold me up to do it."

"It might take more doing than you think," Cason said.

"My goodness," Leonard said, "you must have had an extra bowl of oatmeal this morning."

"You want to be first?" Cason said.

"Hey, Cason," I said. "You look like a guy might be tough, but you mess with Leonard, when they're cutting you open and putting your ruptured liver in a jar, your ghost will still be trying to figure out what truck hit you and when."

Cason looked at Leonard for a long moment. Leonard said, "What he said."

Cason smiled, studied Leonard. "You two are buddies. That is so sweet."

"Yeah," I said, "we're tough, and when times are rough we can sew our own clothes and grow a garden."

"Really?" Cason said.

"No," I said. "But we're tough."

Cason smiled. "All right," he said. "We're all tough guys. It's just that Mrs. Christopher is a friend of the family. Was my third-grade teacher. Her family has money, though she doesn't look like it or act like it. Her dead husband was in oil, and he was in a lot of it. She came to me for help because I used to work for a paper in Houston doing investigative reporting. Now I'm over in Camp Rapture, writing a bullshit column. I decided she needed help that could be on it twenty-four seven, and that wasn't me. Camp Rapture doesn't have a private investigator, but she saw your ad. I was a little reluctant, but I didn't know what else to do for her."

"Good to know we're deeply wanted and widely respected," Leonard said.

"I put those ads in every paper in a fifty-mile radius," Marvin said. "Your paper got me the only response."

"Try the online ads," Cason said. "More people read those these days. I'm lucky I got a job, way newspapers are changing. But, the thing is, I knew a lot of investigators when I worked for the paper in Houston, and I didn't think much of them. They mostly took up time and took up money. So I wanted to make sure you really would look into things."

"You can bet we'll look into them," I said. "Marvin is so honest it hurts our feelings, and we're so honest we hurt our own feelings."

Cason grinned. "Mr. Hanson has my number. You need anything, give me a call. I have a friend who is a bear for research. Maybe we can help you."

"We'll keep it in mind," Marvin said.

Cason put the check on the desk, smoothed it out where he had wrinkled it by pressing his palm across it twice, and went out.

As he closed the door Leonard said, "Please do be careful of the stairs."

When he was gone, I said, "Damn, he's out of our sight, what, three seconds, and I miss him already."

"Too bad he isn't gay," Leonard said. "For him, I could ditch John in a minute. He wears Old Spice. I like Old Spice."

"Frankly," Marvin said, "he's just the kind of guy I'd like to punch in the mouth."

"And," Leonard said, "he's just the kind of guy I'd like to have put something in my mouth."

"One of you is mean," I said, "the other one is nasty."

8

Marvin locked up and we walked downstairs to the lot. The girl in the shorts was no longer visible in front of the bike shop, but I checked just in case.

"Now, what exactly is it we're saying we're gonna do?" I asked Marvin as we walked. "We're all up in Cason's face, and we're all behind you, and we don't even know what we're talkin' about."

"That isn't new for you, is it?" Marvin said.

"Ha. Ha," I said.

"For all we know," Leonard said, "you've signed us up to jack off donkeys at an animal sperm bank."

"And the way I hear it," I said, "you get through with the donkeys and go home, they don't even call or write."

"I'll explain at lunch," Marvin said. "You get the money back?"

"We did," Leonard said, "and a teeny bit more. We figured it wasn't dishonest for him to tip. Mrs. Johnson can use as much of it as she can get."

"What I'm wondering," I said, "is what if Thomas and his friend Chunk want revenge on us or the client?"

"Would they?" Marvin asked.

"Well, one of them is missing a kneecap," Leonard said, "and the other one will have to have his girlfriend pick his nose, wipe his ass, and pull his crank because his hand is kind of swollen up."

"He had it comin'," Marvin said. "The sonofabitch."

"Some people might think the same of us," I said.

Marvin gave me a confused look.

"He's been reading some self-help books or somethin'," Leonard said.

I took the hundred I had taken from Thomas's wallet and gave it to Marvin. "Here's the booty."

"We'll take it to her," Marvin said, and put it in his wallet.

9

The day had started to grow cooler, but not so cool it was uncomfortable. The sky was gray and there were strips of gloomy clouds across it and they had fuzzed out the sun so that it looked like a lightbulb burning behind gauze. In the distance, on the horizon, in line with the street, the sky was darker and I saw a strip of lightning jump and flash away. The rain that had come early in the morning and retreated now had a companion, and it was blowing our way.

We drove in Marvin's car over to Mrs. Johnson's house, which was on the edge of the area where we had been last night. We parked in her gravel driveway and got out. It was a very small house, but brightly painted in a kind of marigold color, and there were flower beds on either side of the little gravel walk. All the flowers were dead or sleeping.

The rest of the neighborhood looked like a war zone.

The house next door was up high on stone blocks, and lying just under it was a dead cat. It had been there long enough to have gone flat and was mostly an outline made of bits of white hair, scattered bones, and a skull. There was just enough flesh on the body to hold it in place. From where the cat was lying, and the looks of the place—a car out front with grown-up grass and a washing machine lying on its side—I had a feeling there wasn't anyone over there looking for their kitty. The cat, like the washing machine, was just part of the landscape to Mrs. Johnson's next-door neighbors. They might have been all-right people doing the best they could, but I got to tell you, you got a dead cat lying in your yard you ought to bury it. That's my motto. No dead animals in the yard for more than fifteen minutes.

"I don't think Fluffy is taking a nap," Leonard said.

"Nope," I said.

At her door, Marvin knocked, and after what seemed like time enough for a new species to have developed from a single cell, the door was answered by Mrs. Johnson. She looked like all the sap had been sucked out of her, she was so small and so wrinkled, but there was a hardness in her eyes that showed her life had been full of experience, and some of it might even have been good. She had a swollen right cheek and a cast on her hand.

"Marvin," she said. "And your boys?"

We were all about the same age, so I found that comment amusing. But I really liked her voice. It was like high cane syrup with a touch of sulfur and a hint of gravel.

"Yes, ma'am," Marvin said, suddenly about twelve years old. "Me and the boys, we got somethin' for you."

Marvin took out his wallet and removed the hundred-dollar

bill and gave it to Mrs. Johnson. She took it and looked at it, said, "I ain't got no change, son. But if you want to go change it, or wait until I can get someone to take it to town—"

"No, ma'am. The fella who stole it, he decided he'd pay a little interest."

"He did, did he?"

"Yes, ma'am."

"You're a terrible liar, Marvin," she said.

"Yes, ma'am."

"You think it's right I take more than he stole?"

"I think you have a cast and that cost money and a hundred dollars doesn't cover it."

"Would you like to come in, sit a spell?"

Marvin said, "No, ma'am, we really can't. We've got some work to do. I don't think you're gonna be bothered again. But, you see him around, or he gives you any reason to feel nervous, call us, and we'll have a talk with him."

"I always see him around," she said. "He lives in the area."

"Yes, ma'am. I know. But . . . Well, you have any cause to worry, you call me."

"All right, dear," she said. "And thank all of you."

Leonard and I smiled and nodded, and turned away, and just before the door closed, Mrs. Johnson said to me and Leonard, "Did you boys hurt him?"

"Yes, ma'am," Leonard said.

"So he didn't like it much?"

"No, ma'am," I said.

"Did you break anything?"

"Yes, ma'am, I believe we did."

"Like what?"

"Well," Leonard said, "I broke his hand, and Hap here broke the other guy's knee and maybe a rib."

"I screamed when he broke my hand," she said. "Did he scream?"

"Yes, ma'am," Leonard said. "And he whimpered too."

She grinned. "But you boys didn't get hurt?"

"No, ma'am," Leonard said. "We came out fine, though I may have strained my elbow a bit on a downswing."

"That Thomas sonofabitch had it comin', breakin' an old lady's hand like that," she said, "and me knowing him all my life. And that Chunk just watchin'."

We went to eat, and then Marvin took us to a coffee shop and showed us the file. It wasn't what I expected. After coffee, Marvin took us to our car, and we didn't say any more about it. Leonard drove me home and went home himself.

10

At home, I thought about what Marvin had shown us in the folder, what he had explained to us. I put my folder on the coffee table in the living room and left it there and walked around the house for a while, then tried to read and tried to watch television, and finally just sat on the couch and watched it get dark and start to rain in a way that made me feel sleepy and gloomy at the same time.

I didn't open the folder again, but that didn't make what was in it leave my head. I thought about it all the time. I was also thinking about that poor dead cat, lying out beside a house where people lived or had lived, and it bothered me they had left it that way.

I went upstairs and stripped down to my shorts and sat by the window. The rain plunked and splattered on the panes so hard I thought they might break. Lightning lit up now and again, and when it did I could see the house next door, appearing to stand behind a stream of bright blue beads, and then the lightning was gone, and it was as if the world had fallen down inside a pit.

I got dressed and went out to the carport and got a shovel from the shed, a rain slicker, an umbrella, and drove over to where the house with the dead cat was.

I got out of the car with my umbrella and shovel, and when I got to where the dead cat lay, I put the umbrella aside. A hard wind was blowing, and when I put it down, the wind rolled it across the yard.

It was maybe midnight and nothing was stirring. I started digging in the yard. I dug a good hole that was long and deep, and then I used the shovel to pry the cat up from the ground. I put it in the hole and carefully covered it and told the cat I was sorry. I got my umbrella and shovel and went back to the car. By the time I put the shovel away I was so wet, rain slicker or not, I was starting to sprout gills.

I still had the stuff Marvin had told us about to deal with. But I didn't have to think about that poor cat anymore. It was down in the ground, wrapped in the earth, not just some hairy outline lying on the grass, pulverized by sunlight and moonlight and savage rain.

When I got home, I undressed and toweled off and lay on the bed naked. I finally slipped under the covers, listening to the rain, the thunder. It sounded good now, not as forlorn as before, but I couldn't sleep.

I thought a little more about what Marvin had shown us, and then I thought about Brett, but that made me miss her. So I thought about something that soothed me as a kid. I was a man in a rocket ship, traveling through space, on my way to a brave new world. I was in a container with a mild unseen, odorless gas that was putting me into suspended animation. I would awake just before arrival and guide the ship in. It would be a world full of beautiful plants and weird animals, but there I would be strong. Like John Carter of Mars my Earth muscles would give me incredible strength and abilities on a world where there was lesser gravity. I would end up with a sword and I would kill monsters and get the girl in the end, and she would look like Brett.

Only problem was, that little trick didn't work this time. I still couldn't sleep.

I got up and put on a CD of selected doo-wop, but that wasn't what I needed and I cut it off halfway through. I settled on *Abbey Road* and *Sgt. Pepper's Lonely Hearts Club Band,* played them through, and when they were done, I turned off the CD player, settled in under the covers, hoping this time I could sleep.

And then I heard a noise. It was a slight noise, a snicking sound coming from downstairs, and then someone gently closing the front door. I got my gun out of the nightstand drawer, and still naked as birth, eased open the bedroom door. A light went on downstairs. I heard the refrigerator door open.

I eased down, slowly. When I got to the bottom stair, I turned and looked in the kitchen. Leonard, wet and dripping, was sitting at the table. He was eating a sandwich and had a glass of milk beside him. A bag of vanilla cookies was open and on the edge of the table. He looked at me, put his hand over his eyes, said, "For heaven sake. Put some clothes on, Hap. I'm trying to eat here. You could make a vulture throw up. That thing looks like a spoiled turkey neck."

11

I went upstairs and put the gun in the drawer and pulled on my pajama bottoms and a T-shirt, slipped into my bunny ear slippers, and went downstairs. Leonard was at the kitchen counter with a loaf of bread and some fixin's, making a fresh sandwich.

"I see my nudity didn't put you off eating my deviled ham," I said.

"Tuna fish," Leonard said. "And I could suggest a better brand."

"You pay for it, I'll buy it," I said, taking a place at the table. "So, what are you doing up at three in the morning eating my food and drinking my milk, and for all I know wearing my underwear and using my downstairs toothbrush? I knew I should have got that key back. I forgot all about it."

"You want a sandwich?"

"Yeah. There's some chips in the cabinet."

"Left side?"

"Yep."

Leonard got the chips down and another plate and made me a tuna sandwich with cheese, light on the mayonnaise, just the way I like it. He made his with mayonnaise and mustard, got the jug of milk out of the fridge, put it on the table and then the sandwiches. He got a diet cola out for me and sat down.

I said, "Just for the record, you are the only one in the universe that has mustard and mayonnaise on tuna, and you don't drink milk with a tuna fish sandwich. Starving people all over the world wouldn't eat mustard on tuna."

"I like milk and mustard on tuna."

"I'm just saying that makes you an alien and universally wrong and you're keeping me up."

He chewed carefully. "I figured since I couldn't sleep you shouldn't, so I came over. Your car, the hood was steaming from the rain. You went out recently. So my guess is you haven't been sleeping so good either."

"Is that really your business?"

"Of course."

I sighed and put down my sandwich. "You remember that dead cat by Mrs. Johnson's house?"

"Yeah."

"I buried it."

"You went out in the rain and buried a dead cat? Anyone see you do it?"

"Don't know, and don't care."

Leonard nodded. "Cookie?" he said, pushing the cookie bag toward me.

I took a vanilla cookie from the bag. Leonard moved the bag to his side of the table, and got up and removed a Dr Pepper bottle from the fridge, sat back down, and twisted off the cap. He took a long swig. "Man," he said. "These are the good ones."

"Right from the warehouse where the originals were made," I said.

"You are the man. Have I ever told you that, Hap? You are the man?"

"Whenever I have something you want me to keep having around, yes, you have told me that."

"Like Dr Pepper?"

"Like that."

"And vanilla cookies."

"Yes."

"Then that whole 'you are duh man' bit has power?"

"A little."

The rain was brutal now. It hit the house hard and the windows rattled. We got ourselves more to drink, turned out the lights, and went into the living room and sat in the dark.

"Isn't this where we say something like 'Well, the farmers need the rain?'" Leonard said.

"I suppose it is."

The file Marvin had given me was still lying on the coffee table. I glanced at it. Leonard glanced at it. We both glanced at it. Neither of us picked it up.

"You ain't been quite yourself for a while, Hap."

"Nope," I said. "I haven't. And you haven't been all that hot since John has been gone."

"Guilty as charged. John's brother is trying to convince him that God can make him straight. His brother says being gay goes against tradition."

"I don't always have turkey on Thanksgiving. That's a tradition. But the world keeps spinning even if I don't eat turkey."

"Yep. It's silly."

A peal of thunder made the house shake.

"Okay," I said. "That makes me think God is on the side of the traditionalist."

Leonard laughed.

12

Here's how it had gone down the day before.

At the coffeehouse, Marvin took out his big folder and gave us each a small folder from inside of it. He had asked that the information be prepared, and Mrs. Christopher, with Cason's help, had done just that.

Marvin said, "Before we open them, let me lay some things out. General information that may or may not be important. Mrs. Christopher is a widow. She has been rich all her life. But not so it shows. She lives simply. Nice home, but nothing flashy. Drives a standard automobile. Inherited money from her husband, who died of a heart attack. She had a nervous breakdown after her son's death, spent some time in a mental institution. Nothing severe. Just there to be watched and evaluated. She came out a couple months later. As far as the death of her son goes, the police believe this is a done deal. That whoever did it is long gone and there's no way to find them. Mrs. Christopher obviously doesn't believe the police know what they're talking about. She believes it wasn't what it appears to be."

"Do you think she's wrong?" I said.

"I'm open to another view if there's evidence to suggest it," Marvin said.

"This Cason Statler," Leonard said. "He seems to believe her."

"Yeah," Marvin said. "But that doesn't mean anything."

"He seems solid enough," Leonard said.

"You just liked the way he looked," I said.

"If he's that pretty, he's honest, and noble, loyal, and trustworthy," Leonard said.

"That's a lot of the Boy Scout oath," I said.

"He wears tight pants and has broad shoulders and is really nice-looking," Leonard said, "so, I thought I'd give him some good attributes."

"I can show you some things in this," Marvin said, tapping his folder, "that are definitely true. So let's pretend this is our first day at school, and we've got our supplies in front of us, and one of those is a nice folder like this one, and I'm gonna be the teacher, and I'm gonna say, Shut up, and open 'em up."

We each opened our folder. There was a photo on top.

"Damn," Leonard said.

The photo had been snapped near a run of water, and at first I couldn't decide what water it was, and then I realized it was the creek that ran by the university at Camp Rapture, wound its way through a very nice park of pecan trees and oaks, and twisted on through the poorer part of town and went on to somewhere beyond my knowledge.

Brett and I had actually gone over to Camp Rapture once to look at a used car. We ended up buying it. I drove our old car, and she drove the one we bought to that park to have a picnic. Brett knew the place and told me about it. I remembered it well. I even remembered that we had tuna sandwiches with bananas cut up in them, along with crushed potato chips. Something Brett came up with. I thought it was a terrible idea until I ate one.

The park was along the edge of a hiking and jogging trail. The trail was wooded on both sides, and beautiful. There were wide spots with picnic tables, and there were big hickory and pecan trees there. We took a walk along the trail. There was a large Hoss apple tree near the edge of the creek. Its thick limbs twisted in unusual ways. We stopped next to it and kissed. The tree was in the photo.

Near the tree, there was woman lying facedown by the side of the trail, not far from the creek. Her hair was dark as sin and her body was pale as bone and she was amazingly thin. Her ribs stuck against her flesh like the framework of a canoe. Her clothes, what looked like shorts, underwear, a bra, and T-shirt, were heaped nearby. All of her clothes were black. Including the underwear.

"Shot in the back of the head," Marvin said. "Name's Mini Marchland. She was on her last outing with Ted Christopher, Mrs. Christopher's son. Turn your page, class."

I lifted up the photo and placed it aside. There was another. A man lying dead on the trail with his face turned to the side. The creek was not visible. He was wearing black jogging shoes, jogging pants, and a dark green T-shirt.

"When did this happen?" I asked.

"Two years ago," Marvin said. "The couple had gone jogging, and when their car was found in the park driveway, and no one came to claim it, people went looking. The bodies lay there for half a day maybe."

"On a jogging trail?" I said.

"That day, the only two people feeling like they needed to be physically fit were these two. They would have ended up better had they sat on the couch in front of the TV at home and ate cheese doodles and sniffed glue."

I looked at some of the other photos. They were more of the same at closer and different angles. There was one close shot of their heads so you could see where the bullets had gone in. Close photos of the girl's clothes heaped up. Close-ups of the ground and shoe marks, and a close-up of Ted's shoe bottoms.

"How did Mrs. Christopher get all of this material?" Leonard asked.

"She knows a lot of people," Marvin said. "And Cason knows a lot of people. Money and connections solve a lot of problems."

"Was the girl raped?" I asked.

"No," Marvin said. "Just stripped. Some of the cops thought maybe he was interrupted."

"If he was," Leonard said, "wouldn't shooting her in the head have been a bigger interruption? Did anybody notice gunfire?"

"Nothing about that in the files," Marvin said. "The guy's wallet was taken."

"He had it in his jogging pants?" I asked.

"That's what they figure. The pants have a back pocket. He didn't have a wallet on him, and there wasn't one in his car. Also, his ring finger was cut off. His mother said he wore a high school graduation ring."

"Did it ever turn up?" I asked. "A pawnshop, that sort of thing?"

"Nope," Marvin said. "Not yet."

"Anything stolen from her?" I asked.

"Her shoes were missing. And her socks."

"Anyone see the couple earlier that day?" I asked.

"Nothing here to indicate that," Marvin said.

"So how did anyone know they went jogging?" I asked.

"When they found the car and found the bodies and jogging clothes, they put two and two together. Jogging clothes. Jogging trail. No brains were overheated in figuring that part out."

"Did you guys notice the bottom of the Christopher kid's shoes?" Leonard said.

We picked up our photos and looked.

"Nice tread," I said.

"Yep," Leonard said, "and I have noticed something that we elite in the crime business like to call a clue."

I turned the picture left and right. I said, "The shoes are clean."

"Yep," Leonard said. "If they were new, and he did a bit of jogging before he got interrupted and shot in the head, maybe they'd look kind of clean, but these look really clean. I think someone at the police department thought the same. Otherwise, why would they take a close-up of the bottom of his shoes?"

"Damn, Leonard," Marvin said, "that may be the first time you've ever had a good idea. You're like a regular Miss Marple."

"And her shoes are missing," Leonard said. "So maybe they got taken away before she was dumped. They got the clothes dropped all right, but forgot the socks and shoes."

"So, you're thinking they weren't shot on the trail?" I said.

Leonard nodded, and now he had about him an air of superiority. That's how he was, one good idea and for a day he thought he was Einstein. "And the car, it could have been left there when the killer dumped them. Or maybe the car was dropped off later. I don't know. It's just an idea."

"It kind of makes sense," I said. "I was bothered by the fact the bodies lay there that long and no one found them. Could have been that way, but I been to that place, and it's pretty busy with people running, walking, picnicking, screwing in the bushes. But if they were killed somewhere else and dropped off early . . . Any information on time of death?"

"They were killed in the morning, was their determination," Marvin said. "That's all the report there is about that. As I said, half a day maybe, if they were lying there the whole time. It's a guess. They're country cops and country doctors. Not stupid, just not geared toward that sort of thing. The place doesn't have a real coroner."

"What about blood evidence?" I asked. "That would let you know something about where they were killed."

"There's no blood evidence information here," Marvin said, shuffling through some pages with writing on them. Leonard and I shuffled through the same pages. I said, "Isn't that a little odd? I mean, they got all this information, but nothing on that?"

"Again, the Camp Rapture police aren't noted for efficiency," Marvin said. "They do have a hell of a fund-raiser with an assort-

ment of different kinds of barbecue, including raccoon and possum, and a country band once a year, but blood evidence tools . . .
not so much. The chief over there is new, and the one before him
was an educated idiot. Degrees out the ass and all the common
sense of a duck. Anyway, the new lady they got is all right. Before
her it was just good old straightforward corruption, so they've
moved up a notch."

"You think this is something the cops of that time were in on?"
I asked. "Some kind of cover-up?"

"I think they were just incompetent," he said.

We sipped coffee, looked at the photos and the information for
a while. When I was through, I looked up, said, "There's a kind of
neatness about it."

"That's what Mrs. Christopher thinks. That it's all too neat."

"What does she think really happened?" I asked.

"She thinks it was a hit," Marvin said. "She thinks he made
someone mad, or knew something he shouldn't, so they killed
him, made it look like another kind of crime. A lot of that is
just motherly instinct, but Cason thinks maybe there's something
to it."

"So you care about what he thinks?" I said.

"He is an investigative reporter. You grow some instincts, you
do that enough."

"And maybe," I said, "Mrs. Christopher is just grieving and
trying to make more sense of this than just a standard old murder.
The idea that anyone can die for any kind of stupid thing is hard to
take, especially if it's someone close to you."

"That's also possible," Marvin said. "The daughter, June, Ted's
sister, thinks there's nothing to it."

"You talked to her?" I asked.

Marvin shook his head. "That will be your job. Mrs. Christopher said Ted and his sister didn't get along well, not even when
they were kids. She also said June was bothered that Mrs. Christopher planned to leave her money to Ted. Which on the surface
sounds tough, but she said she planned to do that because June

married into money and divorced real well. Ted, without family money, would have ended up with the lint in his shorts. I should note too, that the private detective she hired didn't believe it was a hit either."

"So we're sloppy seconds?" I said.

"Yep," Marvin said. "She told me that right up front. I knew the guy she hired, Jimmy Malone. Used to run into him from time to time doing police work. Not exactly on the up-and-up. When he didn't find anything, Mrs. Christopher let it lie for a while, then got it on her mind again that it was a setup, and hired us."

"So," Leonard said, "she thinks Malone took the money and did nothing?"

"My guess is," Marvin said, "that's what Cason thinks and is afraid we're gonna do the same. Me, I don't know. Jimmy was a shit, and a womanizer, and he liked money too much, but he usually did the job. He just didn't always do it the way it ought to be done. He didn't mind playing angles. But the thing is, he didn't find out any more than the police knew."

"We could talk to him," Leonard said.

"Only if you talk to the dead," Marvin said. "He retired, then promptly drowned in a boating accident out at the lake."

Leonard said. "What's this?" He was holding up one of the photos of the dead girl.

"Kind of obvious, don't you think?" Marvin said.

"Not the girl. The tree."

"Let me see," Marvin said. "I'm going to go for Hoss apple."

"The other tree," Leonard said.

"Hickory nut," I said.

"No. What's on the tree?"

We each found our copy of the photo and looked at the hickory tree. There was something on it all right. It was an angled view but it was some kind of drawing. What I could make out was a horned head and a partial face. It was painted there in red. Spray paint, most likely.

"Graffiti," I said.

"Yeah," Leonard said, "but is there anything about it in the notes?"

"No," Marvin said. "And that's because no one thought it meant anything. Kids paint on trees and underpasses and walls all the time. Why would someone kill them and then make a design on a tree?"

"All I'm saying," Leonard said, "is Mrs. Christopher may be right. It might not be a random murder."

"That whole mystery clue thing with paintings on trees and feathers and moles in the shape of the state of Rhode Island on a blonde's ass, in real life, it doesn't happen much," Marvin said.

"He's working his way through the Sherlock Holmes series," I said. "He's gotten a little obsessive about mysteries. He found a pair of socks he's been missing for a couple of months, and he thinks he's full of deductive reasoning now. Like maybe the socks had some kind of plan to hide out."

"Listen, Ace," Marvin said. "You and Hap just go out and ask questions and bumble around. I'll do the real detective work from the office."

"Ouch," Leonard said.

13

So that's how it went. Now we were sitting on the couch looking at those same photos and reading the information that came with them, thinking back on our meeting with Marvin.

It had started raining hard again, and the atmosphere had settled on the house like a woolen cap. The electricity blinked and crackled a few times but stayed on. It was so dark outside we had to turn on a light.

"So," Leonard said. "Where do we start?"

"Same place the cops did, with the people who knew the victims."

"There's a long list here," Leonard said, flipping through the folder.

"I think we should do what Marvin suggested. Talk to the sister."

"To do that," Leonard said, looking out the window at the rain, "we have to get off the couch. And drive around. We could wait until tomorrow."

"We weren't hired to stay home and play Scrabble."

Leonard's eyes lit up. "It's a perfect day for Scrabble. Me and John used to play Scrabble when it rained."

"I'll get us a couple of rain slickers and we'll go to work."

"So," Leonard said, "you're not suggesting we sit on the couch in rain slickers and play Scrabble and call that work?"

"Nope," I said.

"Dang it."

We left Leonard's wreck in the driveway to let the rain work the hardened bird shit off his windshield, took my car.

Before we left, Leonard got something out of his car and slipped in beside me. He laid what he had on the seat between us and pulled off his slicker and put it in the backseat with mine. He picked up what he had laid down and put it on his head.

"What in the hell is that?" I said.

"It's a deerstalker cap."

"A deerstalker cap?"

"You know, Holmes wore one in the movies."

"I know, but what are you doing with one?"

"I'm wearing it."

"Should I wear a bowler and carry an umbrella and let you call me Watson?"

"Would you?"

"Where did you get that?"

"I bought it last Halloween, for a party."

"You dressed up like Sherlock Holmes for Halloween?"

"I don't get to dress up often," Leonard said. "John went as Watson."

"So why are you wearing the hat now? Halloween is long past."

"We're on the hunt. The game's afoot."

"Leonard, you are not wearing that foolish cap."

"Why not?"

"Because you stand out like a hard dick in a nunnery."

Leonard quit looking at me. He turned and stared at the windshield.

"So you're gonna give me the cold shoulder?"

He didn't respond.

"You have this thing for hats, Leonard, but you are not a hat person . . . Look, you can wear it in the car. The car only. Got me?"

Leonard put on his seat belt, rested his hands in his lap, and stared straight ahead.

"Outside the car, you got that thing on I might have to kill you."

14

First on our list was Ted's sister's house. My idea of a really neat house is one that doesn't have to be held up with a stick, and there are no burnt cans in a pile in the driveway or an old Dodge on blocks with chickens roosting under it.

This house was way past that. It was so cool and connected to the center of the universe it stopped raining when we got there. It was behind a fence and a barred gate. As we cruised up, through the gate, we could see there was enough green yard to play the Super Bowl. Even the colorful leaves that fell from the trees and blew across the grass seemed embarrassed by the intrusion.

We parked in front of the gate. I rolled down the window and pushed a button on a metal box inside a brick indentation. There was a buzz and a long silence. I was about to push it again when a snappy female voice with an accent south of the border asked if she could help us.

I explained who we were and what we were doing and that June's mother had hired us to look into something for her. The voice went away. I turned and looked at Leonard. He was still wearing the deerstalker.

The voice came back, said we could come up, but the tone now was sharp and hard enough to clip paper dolls from cardboard. I guess she had hoped we would be rejected.

The gate slid back and we glided in. The driveway was a big loop of shiny wet concrete in front of a yellow adobe house with a Spanish tile roof. The house was big enough and tall enough to hold all of Noah's animals and a spare woodchuck. You could have driven four horses running abreast through any of the windows, and the doorway was tall enough and wide enough to accommodate at least one war elephant if it bent its head slightly and went through politely.

No one rode out to meet us in a golf cart, so after I made Leonard take off his hat, we got out and stepped up the walk. When I looked back at my car, it looked unnatural in the driveway. That driveway knew and adored limousines and sports cars, not functional metal, plastic, and glass. I leaned down by the side of the walk and felt the grass. Damn if it wasn't artificial.

Leonard wanted to ring the doorbell, so I let him. I wanted to ring it too, but sometimes you have to give in to the children. You could hear it chime throughout the house.

No one inside made a rush of things. Of course, a house that big, you might have to pack a sandwich before you went to answer the door.

When the door was finally opened it was the woman that went with the voice over the intercom. She was a petite Hispanic woman in her late twenties and she was actually wearing a maid outfit, just like in the movies. She had beautiful black hair and great skin and lips that looked like they would have been fun to suck on. Because of her stern voice, I had somehow expected her to look like the ass end of a mule and be built like a linebacker.

We were invited inside. I tried not to rubberneck. I had been in government buildings that size, but not a house, and the government buildings weren't so well furnished.

The maid hustled us along a long wide hall with blue and white tile floors. The walls had paintings on them that looked like they had been painted by madmen and recently. I liked them.

We were led off the hall through another war-elephant-size door and into a library that made the one downtown look like a used-book store. The books smelled of leather and old paper and more knowledge than could be acquired in three lifetimes, plus a whiff of cigar smoke covered in a light overcoat of air freshener. The place had a masculine feel about it, with leather couches and chairs and sliding ladders to climb onto to look at books on the upper shelves. There was a large window at the back and looking through it we could see a shiny pond out there, recently swollen by the rain. Beyond that was a wall like out front.

The maid told us to make ourselves comfortable and went away.

We sat on the couch and Leonard said, "Can you believe this is in the center of town? Hidden up here in the trees?"

"I can't believe a place like this is anywhere," I said. "I thought they made this stuff up for the movies."

"The movie screen wouldn't be wide enough to hold this place," Leonard said. "It might take a few theaters just to get that hallway in frame."

A moment later a woman came into the room. She was some woman. She looked like she was dressed to go out on the town, and not our town. Someplace in Manhattan, perhaps Paris, London, or Rome. Her long blonde hair was waved and she wore a pantsuit of shimmering white and she had a small glass in her hand and it was half-filled with a golden liquid that I knew wasn't fruit juice.

"Good afternoon, gentlemen," she said. It was a nice voice full of pep and insincerity. "I'm June. I hope you don't mind if I don't offer you a drink. I thought we could race through this rather quickly."

"That's fine," I said.

She came and sat in a leather chair across from us and put her drink down on the wooden coffee table between us, no coaster. It was a heavily stained table and it was the only thing in the room besides the books that looked old.

"So, you're private detectives," June said, smiling. She had nice teeth and just the slightest bit of an overbite.

"We're not exactly private detectives," I said.

"Oh," she said.

"We've still got the training wheels on," Leonard said.

"So should you be on the job?" she asked.

"We've had a lot of experience," I said. "We're just not what you'd call official. We're operatives. We work for a private detective."

"So someday you may get a little badge, a whistle, and a canteen," she said.

"Our boss," Leonard said, "he started with Where's Waldo books to sharpen us up, but now we've moved on to interviews. We mostly ask short questions."

"I see," she said. She grinned and leaned back and sipped her drink and studied Leonard, then me. Her eyes were very green and very penetrating.

"You boys look a little rough," she said. "Like you've been around the block a few times."

"Maybe more than a few," I said.

"Oh, I didn't mean anything by it. I like the way you look. Most of the men I know use skin cream and have straight noses and the most violent thing they do is grunt playing table tennis. Sometimes, in their sleep, they fart dramatically. Oh, I'm telling, aren't I?"

She moved her head slowly, so we could have a look at her profile, and then she moved it back and sipped her drink.

"It's just that I don't know why my mother is bothering with all this, or why she would send you to talk to me. There's nothing I can add. Ted and his girlfriend were murdered for sex and money. Though they didn't get the sex, and my guess is they didn't get much money."

"Do you know what was actually stolen besides his ring?" I asked.

"Well, he may have had money in the wallet," June said. "But I don't know."

"Credit cards?"

"Most likely. Several. Mostly filled to the brim and leaking over, would be my guess."

"Did the police say anything about anyone trying to use them after his death?"

"No. I know you're thinking that might mean the robbery was a sham. But I think whoever did it panicked and took what was in the wallet and was afraid to use the cards. Afraid they'd be tracked. Or maybe the cards got canceled before the killer could use them, and they just disposed of them."

She leaned back in her chair and crossed her long panted legs and dropped her head slightly. I was sure she knew the effect this had; the way her hair fell across one eye, and the way she looked when she lifted her head and smiled that sexy beaver-toothed grin.

"Look," she said, "my brother, he and I weren't close. I'm sorry about what happened to him, but it was an unfortunate accident.

Wrong place. Wrong time. I suppose it could have been some-one who knew him, knew he was going to be there, thought he had money, and jumped him, but I think he was a victim of opportunity."

"What about the girl?" I asked.

"She was a tramp. And in case you're vague on that, let me translate. She was Miss Insert Slot B."

"That covers a lot of ground," I said.

"And a lot of ground was covered," June said. "Only thing that surprised me about her was that she got killed in the daytime."

"Beg your pardon?" Leonard said.

"She didn't go out in the daytime."

"Fear of skin cancer?" I said. "She freckled?"

"Nope . . . Wait for it . . . She thought she was a vampire."

15

"Big teeth?" Leonard said. "Bite your neck, suck your blood? Wear a cape? Turn into a bat?"

"I doubt she turned into a bat," June said. "A bitch maybe, but not a bat."

"So, you're not denying the cape?" he said.

She smiled at Leonard.

"You knew Mini, then?" I said.

"Some. Liked to wear black and her hair was dyed so dark it looked like strands of shadow. She mainly went out at night. Claimed the sunlight made her weak, unless she needed to go out, and if she did, she seemed spry enough. She was out that day, wasn't she? The day she got popped. She was said to drink blood.

Mostly it was her who said it. She was a goddamn nut. Being a nut was kind of her hobby. Some people collect stamps or keep a diary, she practiced doing nutty things."

"It probably has nothing to do with anything," I said, "outside of it's just weird as all daylights and I want to hear about it, but could you give us some more background on her?"

"I didn't know her well. I didn't want to know her well. But she told me a few things when she got out of jail."

"Jail?" I said.

"Yeah. She and my brother dated for a while, and I was trying to patch things up with him, because, as I said, we didn't get along. So, in the process, me and her hung a little and she talked a lot. I picked up other bits of her story here and there. Mini roosted with a really screwball crowd. Especially Evil Lynn."

"You're yankin' me?" Leonard said. "She had a friend named Evil Lynn?"

"I haven't had the pleasure of yanking you."

She smiled at Leonard seductively. I thought: Lady, you are wasting the possibility of a few wrinkles around your mouth on someone who is seriously batting for another team. Look this way.

She didn't.

"Was Evil Lynn her real name?" I asked.

"Of course not. Her last name was Gonzello. I called her Godzilla, not Evil Lynn. I can't remember Godzilla's first name. Cassie. Candy. Canola. Something like that. Only met her once, at my brother's place, and that was enough. There were several of them, actually. Vampires I mean . . . Let's walk outside. My husband used to smoke cigars in here, and I can still smell them, and him. Both stink."

We walked through the hallway, outside into the backyard. There were trees and a few leaves, and there was a man in work clothes walking around with a stick with a point on the end of it. He was stabbing the leaves and putting them in a big, black plastic bag he was dragging.

"I know a guy works doing special effects in movies," she said.

"I'm thinking about having plastic trees put in. These are so messy."

Leonard looked at me out of the corner of his eye. I looked back and tried not to laugh. Plastic trees?

Underneath one of the pesky real trees was a stone table with a bench on either side. We sat down there.

June rattled the ice in her glass, looked at what was left of her drink as if it were the last of all sunshine, and said, "This is what I know, and all I know. And when I tell you what I know, I don't want to talk about it again. I'm all through. Just thinking about her and her nutball friends makes my ass tired."

She shifted her tired, but very nice, ass on the bench and looked at the pond. There was a big insect, a dragonfly, cruising over the water. She put her focus on that for a while. Maybe she was thinking about having it killed and crucified on the edge of the pond as an object lesson, then having the yard sprayed with insecticide. She could always get her special effects friend to make her a robotic dragonfly, maybe some birds. She drank and moved the liquid around inside her mouth in case her teeth were in need of a whirlpool bath. The man with the pointed stick and the bag full of leaves moved across the yard and around a corner of the house and out of sight.

June swallowed loudly, said, "Mini hooked up with Ted because they were both a little freaky. Ted, he was into anal, and she didn't mind it. His girlfriend before, Lori, not so happy about it. She had two kids, and she told me all Ted wanted to do was crawl up her poop chute. It's all he talked about. Had videos and magazines and a game plan in bed that always, if you'll pardon the pun, ended the same way."

I wasn't sure where this was going, and maybe it was going a little too far south, but Leonard and I let it go. I kind of like nasty stories.

June said, "She started thinking, from the way the kid's toys smelt and felt, that while she and the kids were out, Ted was greasing up and shoving toys up his ass."

"Ouch," Leonard said. "Hope one of those toys wasn't a bicycle."

"So, she confronts him, and he admits it, and she is major pissed off, and he says, 'Hell, just wash them off.' He wasn't concerned. It was all about his ass, his fetish."

"And that was, rim shot, so to speak, the end of the relationship," I said.

"Not yet. She thought maybe he could change. We always think our men can change, and they can't. Assholes at birth, assholes at death. A motto I live by. Anyway, one day she comes home, and she's got the children with her, and what does she find but a drunk and drugged-out Ted passed out in the living room on the rug, naked, with the engine of a hard plastic toy train up his ass, the rest of it dangling out, all the way down to the caboose, like it couldn't make the hill."

"Oh, hell," I said. "That had to hurt."

"Yep. Bled on the carpet. Children were traumatized, and no one wanted to play with the train thereafter. And she'd already dealt with him and a rubber duck and a twirler's baton, so she'd had enough. The train set was expensive. You can buy a duck or a baton anywhere and mostly cheap, but not those buddies. She was fed up with him, and she liked that carpet. Moroccan. Way more expensive than the train. So, it was choo-choo-choo-cha-boogie, you are gone, baby. So, that leads him to Mini, who is connected to Godzilla and a couple other girls who drink blood. Good thing for Ted is, Mini didn't have a problem with the ass business."

"Will there be more trains and tunnels in this story?" Leonard asked.

"No. We're switching tracks," June said. "I'm just trying to say nuts attract nuts. Now we're going to the Children of the Night. That's what they called themselves. Is that hokey or what?"

The maid, as if on cue, came out with another drink, set it on the table in front of June, and without a word went back to the house. I watched her swing away with more than a bit of pleasure. Being male is a full-time, and sometimes tiring, job.

"You like that maid outfit?" June said to me.

"I don't think it would fit me," I said, "but it's very nice. I don't have the legs for it either."

"You ought to see me in one," she said.

"And what days do you wear it?" I asked.

She snorted and sipped her fresh drink. She was starting to get pretty lit, though she was an experienced drunk and wasn't losing her focus on the story, and the words came out clear, if slightly spaced, as if they had to stop and rest before going on.

"I don't know why Mini felt she could talk to me, but she did. Maybe she needed to get away from all weird all the time. Also, she was drunk and at a party here at my house, and she was fresh out of jail and no one else wanted to talk to her. Word gets around. Had I not been drunk, I wouldn't have wanted to talk to her myself. She told me she and these other girls, Godzilla, as ring-leader, would go out to the cemetery and have ceremonies, reading spells out of witchcraft books, lighting candles, that kind of crap, calling on Satan to come on up and see them sometime. Then one night, Godzilla's girlfriend . . . Let's see . . . She was called Trip. I don't know what her real name was, but she was called that . . . So, one night, they're in the cemetery, and they're doing some ceremony or another, and it leads to Trip letting Godzilla cut her neck a little with a pocketknife and suck blood from the wound. And then everyone has to have a taste, so there's more cutting. Everyone giving up a little blood, except Godzilla. They all take turns sucking neck, which I figure is pretty damn unsanitary.

"Godzilla and Trip, who were lesbian lovers, end up making out. Then the nonlesbians say what the hell, and they're all making out, followed by more blood sucking. Anyway, they're sucking blood and suckin' whatever, and Godzilla, who was a pretty tough-lookin' broad, or seemed that way the time I saw her . . . I figured about three feet of chain and two stiff drinks and I could have whipped all of them."

"And without the chain?" I said.

"Might have been touch and go," June said.

"So you were saying?" I said.

"Well, they were doing vampire things, I guess. But Mini, she tells me that the night in the graveyard when everyone got naked and tried to find a place to bite, Godzilla started talking about killing people. Feasting on their blood, as she put it. Mini thought it was cool talk, but just talk. Like you know, when you say you're putting a band together in your garage and you're going to cut a record and go all the way to the top, and you know you're not, and the best that happens is you end up playing a bad version of 'Wipe Out' or 'Free Bird' at a bar for tips. Anyway, Mini claimed she was just playing along. Told me she thought she was a vampire on the weekends and late at night, and the rest of the time, she had to work at RadioShack. The other girls, they all had money and time to waste. Harder to be a vampire when you have to be nice to customers and earn a paycheck."

June took a long ice-rattling drink from her glass. When she started talking again her tongue had grown a little thick.

"What happened was, one night they're driving along in Godzilla's car, four of them, Godzilla, Trip, Mini, and this other goober I can't think of, and they come across this drunk frat-rat on a bicycle. Mini said they could see him pedaling along ahead of them. He was all over the road, like a sidewinder snake trying to drive a tricycle. So they pull over and get out, and this guy, he thinks he's hit the jackpot. Four hotties giving his drunk ass attention. Well, three hotties and Godzilla.

"They get him to abandon his bicycle, which he tells them he stole off a front porch, and he climbs into the car. Mini said Trip showed him some tit and a bottle of whiskey, and now this sap thinks he's died and gone to heaven."

Something clicked while June was talking. I remembered this. I had seen stuff about it on the local news, a while back. The vampire angle had been mentioned, but I had forgotten all about it.

"They drove over to Camp Rapture, teasing him and giving him whiskey, and then Mini said Godzilla said something about her and Trip taking the boy out behind the warehouse district and doing him a favor. By this point, this guy was so drunk and worked up he'd have humped a crippled sheep wearing stockings, a garter belt, and a purple beret. To him, even Godzilla was probably starting to look like a runway model. Man, where's my maid? I need another drink."

"Finish your story," I said, "and I'll look her up for you."

June held up her glass and shook the ice in it, hoping the maid might hear. She didn't. June shook the glass harder. After a moment she gave up and placed it on the table and burped pleasantly with her hand almost making it over her mouth.

"There's not much left to tell," June said. "They took him out back of a shed, down in the warehouse district. Mini said she could see what was happening from the inside of the car. They were a ways back, but it was all in full view. While the guy is shucking his drawers, thinking he's going to get to churn the log in the mill, out of her purse Godzilla pulls a big knife and sticks the guy in the neck."

June made a stabbing motion in the air, gritting her teeth as she did.

"Then Godzilla pounced on him, started sticking him, lots of times. He screamed and fell down on his face. Godzilla kept after him. She wasn't any slacker. She tried to hand Trip the knife, but she wouldn't take it. Godzilla went back to it. Trip went back to the car and got in and sat there and all she could say was that there was a hole in the guy's back big enough to shove a wiener dog through. Or so Mini said. They watched Godzilla bend over the body and start sucking at the blood.

"When it was over, Godzilla came back covered in gore. Mini said her eyes were wide and bright and she had that big wet knife in her hand and a loopy blood-smeared smile on her face like she'd just had a seven-course dinner and someone had been polite enough to burp her.

"Mini said right then she was through playing vampire. She got out of the car and made a run for it. And when she looked back,

Trip was out of the car and chasing after her. But Trip, drunk, or just worn out by shock, fell down in a stretch of trees, and Mini just kept going. They were way out in the country, so she got lost. Wandered through some woods and over a little creek, finally saw lights. It was Camp Rapture. She could see the university tower all lit up."

June paused and closed her eyes. The last words she had spoken had begun to have fuzz around them. I said, "So, she saw the tower lit up."

"Real pretty, that tower at night," June said.

"Yeah, it's nice," Leonard said. "What happened after Mini saw it?"

"She went into town and found the police and told them about it. They went out, and sure enough, they found the guy. He looked like bloody rags, he was so cut up. And when they found Godzilla and Trip and the other girl back at Godzilla's pad, Godzilla was still covered in blood.

"They arrested all of 'em, includin' Mini. But it was decided she didn't do anything but hang out with the wrong crowd, so they let her out of jail and told her to hang up her gothic duds and turn state's evidence. She did. Oh, God. I'm drunk. Do I sound drunk?"

"Amazingly," I said, "not much."

"Godzilla had somehow dropped her credit card, near the body, so when they found the body they found the card, and that established the likelihood of her being there. Later all the girls turned on her, even Trip. That put the nail in her coffin, which, for a vampire, seems appropriate. But there was one more thing. Godzilla threw up when she was arrested. All that blood. Samples were taken. Eventually, the results came back. It was the guy's blood, of course. She actually had sucked down about a half quart of it, the greedy whore."

"Do you remember the dead boy's name?" I asked.

"Shit," June said, "I'm two sips off startin' to have a hard time rememberin' my own name. All I know is the family was a good family out of Houston, and they were in court during Godzilla's trial. I heard rumors Godzilla swore she'd get all the other girls, kill them, or have them killed. But I heard one of my cousins say he saw Bigfoot once, and I just got to take him at his word."

"And how are the girls?" I asked.

"How the hell would I know?" she said, put her head on the table, closed her eyes, and in a moment she was snoring like a water buffalo.

"Well," Leonard said. "Reckon that's our cue."

16

We went back into the hall and the maid met us there. She was friendlier now and her voice was less gruff. She said, "She drunk yet?"

"Yes, but she went down a pretty clear talker," I said.

"Passed out?" the maid asked.

"Yep," Leonard said.

"She's like that. Talks almost like she hasn't had a drink, then she's snoozin'. You got to watch sometimes so she doesn't bump her head, she'll go down so fast."

"We'll take that under advisement," Leonard said.

"You know, in spite of what she says, she loved her brother very much."

"So, you been listening in?" I said.

"Absolutely. I knew she wanted another drink too, but I didn't bring it. She didn't need it. "

"We heard she was pretty upset about her mother leaving the money to the brother," Leonard said.

"Not really," the maid said. "She was worried that Mini would get her hands on it. She didn't want that to happen, and that's all there was to that. I've worked for her for five years, and she's not as heartless as she can sound when she's drunk. She and her brother didn't get along, but she loved him. She just didn't know how much until he was dead. I'll walk you gentlemen out."

Outside, Leonard said, "That's some story."

"Actually," I said, "I remember hearing about the case on the news. I don't remember the details, but I remember hearing about it."

"Me too," Leonard said. "But it happened before Mini bit the big one, and before she was dating Ted, so I'm not sure it means anything, even if those girls could actually change into bats."

"No one said they could change into bats," I said.

"I know, but that would be way cool, wouldn't it?"

"Oh, yeah," I said, and we bumped fists. "Do you think Mini telling June about all that in such detail means anything other than they were both drunk?"

"Got me," Leonard said.

Back in the car Leonard put on the deerstalker.

"You're just jackin' with me, aren't you? You know you look like a moron, but you're wearing that thing to get my goat and all its children, aren't you?"

Leonard leaned over and adjusted the car mirror and looked at himself. "I think it fits my personality."

"What personality?"

"That's just mean, Hap."

I put the mirror back the way I liked it. "We'll take back streets," I said.

"I want a Sonic burger."

"You have money?"

"Not on me . . . You have money?"

"Yes."

"Will you buy me a burger?"

"Will you take off the hat?"

"You can eat in the car at Sonic."

"Yes, but the waitress who brings it out will see you and know I'm with you."

"No one will know you."

"It's not a chance I'm willin' to take."

"I hate you," Leonard said.

17

In Marvin's office, Marvin looked up some things on the Internet and made a few calls to cops, a warden, some prison guards, and other people, including a sandwich shop that delivered.

He didn't offer us a sandwich, nor did he offer to let us order our own.

Leonard, wearing the deerstalker, sat in a client chair reading one of Marvin's fishing magazines. I sat with my hands on my knees feeling like a bored kid.

After a long while, Marvin put the phone down, scribbled some notes, said, "Okay, I remember this vampire case. I checked some of the details, and it appears June is pretty accurate in her story. I just didn't put Mini together with it, didn't remember her name and Mrs. Christopher didn't mention it."

"It seemed too coincidental to ignore," I said.

"It damn sure looks like the vampire killings and Mini go together," Marvin said. "It also appears that—"

Marvin paused and looked at Leonard. "You know, Leonard, if I'm going to talk seriously, and you're going to listen seriously, you have to take off that goddamn shitty hat."

"Thank you," I said.

"Et tu?" Leonard said.

"Now he's trying to show some education," I said.

Marvin just looked at him.

Leonard slowly removed the hat and placed it on his knee. "All my life people have been jealous of me."

"Keep tellin' yourself that," Marvin said. "So, what June told you, it's pretty much right. We'll just have to take her word on her brother and the toy train."

"Oh, man," I said. "That was something I could have gone to my grave without knowing."

Marvin nodded. "Yep. Me too. What June didn't tell you, and probably doesn't know, but what my phone calls just found out, is about two weeks ago, Evil Lynn, real name Ray Lynn Gonzello, Godzilla to June, had a prisoner start somethin' with her over who knows what. Godzilla beat her down like she was tenderizin' meat. Then she challenged a fellow ass-whipped prisoner to cut her. Let her get to the shiv she'd just taken away from her. Wanted to show her that it wouldn't hurt. That any wound she got would heal. That she was in fact a vampire."

"Uh-oh," Leonard said. "This isn't going to end well."

"On the nosey," Marvin said. "Fact was she didn't heal up at all. Got stabbed under the armpit and bled out faster than you could say 'Oh, shit. I've been stabbed under the arm and it hurts like a motherfucker.' According to what I got here, Godzilla had some actual last words."

"I'm guessin'," said Leonard, "it's not the stuff about 'Oh shit, I've been stabbed under the arm.'"

"Kind of sad, really," Marvin said. "She said, 'I'm just a girl.'"

"Nothing like experience to put things into perspective," I said.

"What I'm thinkin'," Marvin says, "is every day she's eating crappy food in the cafeteria, and she's not suckin' blood—I don't think—and she's behind bars like a zoo animal, no vampire powers at work, and she still didn't get it. That's the part amazes me."

"The knife was the only kind of explanation she understood," I said.

"Now here's some more CliffsNotes. A year back, Trip, real name Tammy Trip, the vampire's assistant, was found dead in her apartment, hanging from a doorway. Drove a big nail there, attached a short noose made of two woven nylon stockings, and hung herself. She was all dressed up in her best black duds. Course, according to my buddy over in Camp Rapture who works for the cops, cop who found her said she had shit herself and her tongue was hanging out so far and so thick, they thought she had a partially deflated balloon in her mouth."

"Dressin' up don't help much," Leonard said, "if you end up with shit down your legs."

"Six months ago, one of the other girls, one who stayed in the car with Mini, name was Joan Carter, was found in her bedroom with a hypodermic needle no longer full of heroin in her arm. She had been dead a few days. Her dog ate most of one of her legs and a large chunk out of her naked ass, but was kind enough to do all his pissin' and shittin' in one corner of the room."

"Leonard can't even do that," I said.

"Then we go back to Mini and her boyfriend," Marvin said. "They were killed two years ago."

"Seems like belonging to or being associated with the vampire clan brings a person bad luck," I said.

"Yep," Leonard said. "But I do have a suspect. Van Helsing."

Marvin ignored that. He said, "Now, I hate to tell you this part, and I suppose when I do, Leonard, you can put the deerstalker back on. Cop over in Camp Rapture tells me that a bunch of them thought from the start the bodies of Mini and Christopher's boy had been killed somewhere else and dumped. And it wasn't the first time they'd seen the devil head symbol, but all of that was kept hush-hush."

Leonard put the hat on, lounged loosely in his chair. "Yeah, baby," he said.

"So the cops weren't as stupid as we thought," I said.

"No," Marvin said. "They thought they'd keep some things back, something they could use to nail their guy later on. Not let it be known they were onto the right idea. Of course, it didn't help. The cases still went cold."

"Are you about to tell us the Devil Red symbol was at the scenes of their deaths?"

"It was found in the apartment where the girl hung herself. It was marked above the doorway where the noose was fastened. Other girl, one with the needle . . . It was drawn on the headboard of the bed. Small, but in sight if you were looking. And, lastly, as you noted, Leonard, it was drawn on one of the trees where Mini and Ted's bodies were found. Since the murders took place in different towns, and some time apart, no one put it together right away. Maybe it should have been obvious, the girls being part of the vampire group. But, different towns, different departments. Mini was killed in Camp Rapture along with Ted. Godzilla in prison—and there wasn't any symbol there, which means she may not have been part of the pattern at all, just stupid. Trip was in LaBorde at the time, having just moved there, and Joan, the dog's lunch, died in Tyler. They figure the killer is spacing his victims out to keep from being connected, to avoid expectations, or is playing a kind of game. Wants to taunt the authorities, show how clever he is. Thinks he's smarter than everyone else."

"And so far," I said, "that's been true. But whoever is whacking them is leaving the devil head symbol, so they're not hiding that hard."

"Here's something else. Mini was about to inherit enough money to not only buy some plastic vampire teeth, but on top of that there would be eight million dollars left over."

"Holy shit," Leonard said, "she invent a perpetual motion machine?"

"Nope. Her mother won the lottery."

18

"That's some lottery," I said. "Eight million dollars."

"Poor girl," Marvin said. "She never got to spend her inheritance." Marvin picked up the notes he had made, glanced at them, and continued. "Her father died when she was young. Her mother remarried, and the old gal wasn't exactly tip-top in the high value department. A drunk. A bit of a whore. Picked up for shoplifting a couple of times. Even had Mini in on the job once, teaching her to stuff items down her pants. And the kid was five. Mother was fired from a lot of jobs, mostly for not showing up, or showing up drunk, and once for giving another employee head in the back room for fifty dollars. She also paid a fine for dumping a dog beside the road and wishing it good luck in the future."

"Everything but wearing polyester jumpsuits," Leonard said.

"The sources for all this reliable?" I said. "We didn't have this info before."

"I wouldn't use them if they weren't," Marvin said. "They don't know it all, but they know a lot. Mostly from cops and retired cops, a couple of lawyers who are only partly shark. But it's just background stuff, nothing that solves anything. It just means all that money might somehow have been a motive. Figuring out if it was or wasn't, that's our job."

"Shit," Leonard said. "I was hoping someone else had done the work and we'd be through after today."

"Actually, that vampire business opened the gate," Marvin said. "Gave me an idea of who to contact on the force over there. Once I knew stuff they didn't, they were more forthcoming with things I didn't know. They figured they might as well tell me. The case was cold to them. So, I hate to give you guys a compliment, but you did good. It's the way it works in the detective business: The more you know, the more others are willing to tell you."

Marvin returned the notes to the table and leaned back in his chair. His chair was much better than ours. It was comfy and had wheels on it. "Mini didn't have true friends because her personality was a little strange. That's why she latched onto the vampire business, got in with that crowd."

"She was pretty," I said. "I could tell that in the photo. A little still, a little pale, and way too dead, but no discernible ants or maggots or signs of rot, still pretty until the bloating. Usually, pretty girls are popular. When they're alive, anyway."

"She was popular with some in a certain way," Marvin said.

"Local hole punch?" I said.

"Yep," Marvin said. "According to Will Turner, a retired cop I talked to, guy who actually interviewed Mini first, after Godzilla did the chop and suck thing. He got the impression that Mini was trying to fit in. Boys liked her for the drawer shuckin' part, but not for too much else."

"If only she could have yodeled," Leonard said.

"You are a heartless sonofabitch," I said.

"I was thinkin' she and her buddies killin' that drunk frat rat was the heartless part," Leonard said. "And as a reward, her mother wins eight million dollars for buying a two-dollar ticket. What's up with that?"

"Bought the ticket at a filling station," Marvin said. "When she got some of the money, she went out to get drunk in celebration, leaving her husband home with a glass of milk and a bologna sandwich. She got so drunk she fell asleep in her car on the railroad track."

"I see this coming," Leonard said.

"She didn't," Marvin said. "A train knocked her ass about two miles down the track and into some woods and into a sink of water. Next morning they found the car. Someone finally saw the roof of the car sticking out of the water, shining in the sunlight. She turned out to have a car engine stuck up her ass. But the good news, my contact said, was the air bag opened."

"That technology," I said, "it's somethin'."

"I presume the husband inherits?" Leonard said.

Marvin shook his head. "Nope. Mini's mother, Twilla, bought herself a new car and a hairdo and about three thousand dollars' worth of duds on credit, then went to a lawyer and made a will. She left it to her daughter should anything happen to her. This was two weeks before Mini was found dead. Little later, Twilla got hit by the train. Not long after, the daughter and the boyfriend bit it."

"Was anyone next in line for the money after Mini?" I asked.

"The animal shelter," Marvin said. "She liked cats. Not dogs, just cats."

"Prejudice is an ugly thing," Leonard said.

"Bert, her husband, wasn't completely left out. He got ten thousand. But that had to bite his butt. Him with ten thousand and the cats with almost eight million dollars. That buys a lot of catnip."

"So Bert could have a grudge," I said.

"I guess the cats are looking over their shoulders," Leonard said.

"Cops looked into him," Marvin said, "up one side and down another. They couldn't find anything that led them to think he was involved or did anything himself. But it's a motive. I don't know how it would connect to the other girls, but maybe he was trying to make it look like the murders were connected with what Godzilla and the girls had done. According to what I got here in my notes, Bert wasn't big enough or tough enough to do much but give Sharon's cats to the animal shelter. That was about the extent of his mean as far as the cops can see. Still, we won't take him off the suspect list."

"June might have a place on that list too," Leonard said. "I don't know how much I buy the 'she really loved her brother' bit. She didn't like the idea that he might get that inheritance instead of her. She had the money to make a hit, and if Mini was there when it was set up, so be it. Not that June needs the inheritance, but the ones who don't need it are often the ones who want more of it."

"All right," Marvin said. "June's on the list too."

"Do you think it's odd that Mini's mom made out a will right after getting the money?" I said.

"Not really," Marvin said. "She was old enough to think about it. Maybe she finally felt motherly and thought if anything happened to her, Mini would get it and she would check out making up for not being the best mom in the world. And if Mini died, well, there was the animal shelter. The husband did hire a lawyer on contingency to try and pry the money from the fuzzy little paws of all those desperate kitties. I don't know how that worked out. But there's nothing about Bert that has to mean murder. And the mother, well, I figure too much alcohol and a big case of the stupids did her in."

I glanced over at Leonard and his deerstalker. I turned to Marvin. "Do you come across many murders where a fella didn't like his best friend's hat?"

"No," Marvin said, looking at Leonard, "but I can understand the impulse."

19

Marvin gave us some contact information for people we might want to talk to, and I folded that up and put it in my coat pocket. We left when his sandwich arrived. We knew when we weren't wanted.

At my place we fried up some egg sandwiches and sat on the couch and turned so we could look at each other. Leonard had finally taken off the deerstalker, so it was easier to do.

We decided we had to see Mini's stepdad, Bert. I called the cell number we had for him. The phone rang awhile, but finally he answered.

I told him we were investigating his stepdaughter's murder, that the mother of Mini's boyfriend had hired us, and could we meet up with him.

"Can't we just talk over the phone?" he said.

"I suppose, but we'd rather do it in person."

"Not anything I can tell you, and since I don't know you, I ain't wantin' you to come out to the house."

"Okay."

"I've had threats."

"Threats?" I asked.

"That's all I'll say about it."

"Look, I don't know about the threats, but we're on the up-and-up. What say we meet someplace public? We'll buy you lunch."

"Made a sandwich already."

"Well," I said, "how about just meeting you in town?"

He was silent for so long I thought the connection was broken. But just when I was about to give up, he said, "I'm going out to the auction barn, catch me there."

"Not sure what you look like."

"Call my goddamn cell, man. Use your head. When you get there, call me."

On the way out to the auction barn, I said, "He sounds paranoid."

"Doesn't mean someone's not after him," Leonard said.

"Take off the hat, Leonard. Where we're going is cowboy country. You going in there looking like that, you're asking for trouble. Only thing missing is a purse."

"This is anything but effeminate," he said. "In Merry Ole England they wore these to hunt deer. Real men. Real guns. Real deer. And this hat."

"Deer probably laughed themselves to death."

When we got out to the auction barn, the parking lot was full of pickups and trailers and everything smelled like animal shit; it was so thick you almost had to climb over the reek to get to the auction barn.

Inside, the place looked like an ad for chewing tobacco and blue jeans. Cowboy hats floated on the crowd, and there was a lot of crowd. Last time I'd seen that many people was in a rerun of *The Ten Commandments*. Who knew cows were that exciting. The animal crap smell was now so intense I felt I needed mountaineer equipment to scale it.

We started moving in among them, and as we went, Leonard pulled the deerstalker out of his back pocket, unfolded it, and popped it out like a wet towel and put it on.

"You sonofabitch," I said.

20

As we rambled through the crowd, a tall cowboy with a hatband full of toothpicks watched Leonard pass with open curiosity. I was right behind Leonard. I said to the cowboy, "He's working a child's party after this."

The cowboy looked at me and nodded, like that explained everything.

We found a spot with a break in people, and went there. I took out my cell and called.

"Yeah," Bert said.

"This is Hap Collins. I spoke to you earlier."

"What about?"

I was more than a little certain now that Bert was not the sharpest knife in the drawer.

"Your stepdaughter. You told me to call."

"Oh, yeah. I'm over by the door. Too many people in there, and hot."

"Okay," I said. "Meet you there. What's your description?"

"What's yours?"

"There's two of us. I'm about six foot with brown hair, stocky. The guy with me is black—"

"Black?" He seemed surprised.

"Yeah. There's a whole race of them. He's just one of them."

"Black, huh."

"Now and always."

There were actually a few black cowboys scattered about the barn, but they had on the proper duds. I said, "You'll know us because he's bigger than me and has gray at the temples. Oh yeah, he's got on a funny hat."

"Hey," Leonard said.

21

It was hot in the auction barn, and it felt good to come out into the open air. There were a number of men and women in cowboy hats and gimme caps out there, and a few of them were smoking cigarettes. One was wiping cow shit off his boots, scraping them over the edge of a concrete step.

That guy, the shit scraper, turned and looked at us. He smiled when he saw Leonard. I had a suspicion he was Bert. He was tall and strong-looking in a working man sort of way; had long muscles and a face that had seen too much sun, and maybe too many fists.

"Damn, man, that is the ugliest goddamn hat I ever seen," Bert said, coming over, pushing his cowboy hat back on his head. "You just wear that to crap in?"

I thought, Bert, my man, you are taking your life into your own hands. Leonard stood there with his hands in front of him, right folded over left, at his belt buckle. That was how he stood when he wanted to look casual but was ready to knock your head off.

Leonard said, "Naw, I crap in cowboy hats. This I keep clean."

Bert and Leonard looked at each other. Bert looked like a tough hombre. Thing was, though, Leonard was a tough hombre.

I said, "Bert, we're just trying to find out who killed your daughter."

"Stepdaughter," he said. "Could have been anybody."

"So no idea?"

"I got an idea."

"And?" Leonard said.

"Keeping it to myself."

"You tell the cops what you thought?" Leonard asked.

"Nope."

"Why not?" I said.

"Didn't care for Mini much. A real weird one and a bitch. Don't like her mother much now. Left her money to the daughter, then to a bunch of fuckin' cats. How about that? Cats. What the fuck are cat's gonna buy?"

"Cat toys," Leonard said.

Bert gave Leonard a look.

"And there's catnip," Leonard said.

"Listen, I don't really care I talk to you guys or not," Bert said.

"What if there was money in it?" I said. I wasn't sure where I was going with that, but I had a hunch Mrs. Christopher might be willing to put out a few dollars for information.

"That depends," I said.

"On what?" Bert said.

"The quality of the information," Leonard said, just like he knew what I was thinking. And he probably did.

"Well, money talks, and bullshit walks," Bert said. "You two don't exactly look like fucking Fort Knox."

"We're not talking about our money," I said.

"How much of the other fella's money, then?"

"Again, that depends," I said.

Bert let that run through his head, which I considered was an easy task.

"I don't know," he said. "I got a feeling I say too much I might get in trouble."

"With who?" I said.

"That's my business."

I could see he was actually nervous, but was waffling on the matter.

"How about I give you a card," I said, "and you call us if you change your mind. This offer is short-term."

"How short-term?" he asked.

"How about tomorrow morning," Leonard said.

"I think you'd take it two weeks from now," he said.

"And I think you don't know us too well," Leonard said.

I took out my wallet and opened it up and took out a card. I gave it to him.

He looked at it, then at me. "Hanson Investigations. Well, if you're Hap Collins, then you must be Hanson."

"Nope," Leonard said. "We work for Hanson."

"You change your mind, call us," I said.

Bert turned the card around and around in his hands. He was giving it serious thought. Finally he put the card in his shirt pocket. He said, "I'll consider on it."

And then he turned and walked away, across the parking lot. We watched until he got in a black truck so old I didn't know what decade it was from. He cranked it, and we kept watching while it coughed smoke and rattled away like something broken tumbling downhill.

"You have cards?" Leonard said. "I don't have any cards."

"Marvin gave them to me."

"He didn't give me any."

"He told me to tell you we would share."

"How are you sharing if you're carrying the cards and I don't have any?"

"I'll share for the both of us," I said.

Driving back to my place, I said, "What do you think?"

"I don't know," Leonard said. "He's an odd one. He's either paranoid, or has delusions of his own importance, or he knows something and he didn't tell us. And what he knows he's trying to turn into money. Maybe with someone else, and us, but the some-one else may be someone he shouldn't have messed with. I think he may actually have been afraid. He was acting tough, but—"

"He was overacting," I said.

"Yep, we ought to know. We do it all the time."

22

Back home, upstairs in the bedroom, I called Brett on my cell. She answered on the first ring.

"So, just sitting around waiting for me to call?" I said.

"Actually," she said, "I'm sitting around in case my boyfriend calls."

"Is he handsome?"

"Not particularly, but he looks great by phone."

"Is he hung?"

"Nope, but I can dream."

"This boyfriend, would he be me?"

"He would."

"Thanks for lifting my spirits."

"You know I love you, even with all your deficiencies."

"How are things?"

"Well, pretty good for a small-blown crisis, but it's the same crisis," Brett said. "The one where my daughter is leading a screwed-up life, but pretends she wants to change and tells me all her woes, then goes right back to doing what she's always done, being who she always was and is. A whore who drinks too much and buys her clothes at expensive stores in Houston, and her underwear at Wal-Mart."

"And you're thinking it's your fault?"

"Some of it is my fault. Except for the Wal-Mart underwear . . . Oh, hell. Who am I talking to? You know I buy mine there too."

"Your ex had a little to do with Tillie's problems."

"True, but I didn't have to set his head on fire. I think it set a bad example."

"Maybe a little," I said.

"Are you doing okay in the private detective business?"

"Well, I'm in it. And there's supposed to be a big check at the end of the rainbow, and me and Leonard got to hear some neat stuff about vampires, devil heads, a dog-eaten body, and a white trash winning the lottery and getting hit by a train. Oh, and a bunch of cats inherited the lottery money."

"Say what?"

I told her all that I had learned.

When I finished, Brett said, "That's some weird stuff."

"You think? When are you coming home?"

"Tomorrow. I'll be home by noon."

"Really?"

"I just made up my mind. Tillie was the same before I got here, and she'll be the same after I leave."

"How is the prostitute business?"

"Booming. One of her johns asked me if I wanted to pull a mother and daughter."

"No shit?"

"Yeah, I made three hundred dollars and there was a pony involved."

"Is that all you made? The pony factor alone was worth three hundred."

23

Leonard was about his business that night, which I thought might be trying to call John and talk him into coming back. I figured Leonard was close to the end of his rope on that. He was sticking with John better than anyone before, but I knew him well enough to know he had a destination in mind, and once he arrived there, if John came back to him bare-ass naked swinging his dick, Leonard wouldn't be interested anymore. Once he cut you loose, he cut you loose.

Me, I pined over everything, worried about everything. I was worrying now. I was worrying that Bert wouldn't call. I was thinking if he did, he wouldn't know anything and that he would just try to work us for money. I was thinking me promising money was stupid. I was thinking I could dip into my savings and come up with a few thousand, if I had to, but I didn't want to, and I didn't want to spend the client's money either.

I was also thinking Bert was just a dumb goober with a brain full of imaginary foes. A man shot down by disappointment, thinking about those cats with his dead wife's lottery money, as if they actually held it in their little furry paws.

I went upstairs and crawled into bed with nothing on but my underwear and read from a good book until midnight. Then I put the book down with only one chapter to go.

I put it down because I was thinking about things that had come at me sideways, out of the past. I don't know what sent them to the forefront, but this sort of thing had been happening for a while. All I could think about when things got quiet was the violence I had done in my life, or been around. Gunfire and fistfights, blood and gray matter splattered on the wall. The way it hit me right then, it was like I had looked in the wrong direction while crossing a road and had been hit by a truck.

I found that I was even breathing rapidly.

I twisted so I could sit on the bed and put my feet on the floor. I took some deep breaths. I tried to imagine encasing my thoughts in a dark balloon and letting it float away.

I had to float a lot of balloons.

After a little while, I felt better. I decided to take a hot shower and stand and soak the back of my neck for a while. I did that, and when I came out, toweling off, I checked the clock for the time. It was late.

I looked at my cell lying on the nightstand.

I had missed two calls.

I checked.

They were from Bert.

24

There was a message on the cell.

"Hey, this is Bert. Saw you and the colored guy with the silly hat at the auction barn, today, remember?" the message started, like maybe we wouldn't remember him. "Give me a call, you got some money. I got something for you."

I called his number.

Nothing.

I left a message.

I had missed his call by only a few minutes. Where the hell was he?

I finished drying off and crawled back into bed and picked up my book. I read only a page or two before I called him again.

Nothing.

I finally turned in and went to sleep, and in the middle of the night I woke up thinking about Bert's call. There was no reason to suspect anything odd, anything foul. He had called and left a message, and I had called back and left one, and that was it, but I couldn't get the paranoid feeling out of my head that something was wrong.

He hadn't said anything particularly suspicious in his call, but I had detected a worried tone in his voice. Or had I? Maybe I was projecting.

I rolled over and tried to go back to sleep, but that didn't work.

I turned on the light by the bed and tried to read some more, but my mind wouldn't focus on the words. I got up and dressed and drove over to Camp Rapture and the address I had for Bert. It was about a forty-five-minute drive.

His place was off the main road and over a cattle guard, down a drive that was little more than a crease in a pasture. As I turned into the long drive, a car nearly sideswiped me, and was gone.

I couldn't tell much about the car, but I thought it was some kind of SUV. All I had seen was lights, and the blur of a passing vehicle. It could have been any dark color.

I drove on cautiously, came to where he lived, which was a green-and-white trailer up on blocks in a little grown-up yard next to a creek on one side, an aluminum outbuilding with the door missing on the other side. I could see a lawn mower in there and what looked like an automobile engine up on sawhorses.

Bert's trailer didn't look as if it had been new when it was new. His pickup was in the yard. The closest house around, another mobile home up the road, wasn't close at all. Maybe half a mile. It was a lonely kind of place.

I sat in my car for a moment, then reached over and opened the glove box and got my .38 Super out of there, along with gloves and a little pocket flashlight. I mention it was a Super because if I don't Leonard always says something like "They don't actually make thirty-eights in automatic." And I always think if they don't, then why do they call it a .38 with a word behind it? Shouldn't he know I'm talking about a .38 Super? Gun fanatics make my ass tired.

This was the sort of thing I thought about when I didn't want to think about doing what I was about to do, because I knew it was stupid, more stupid than Leonard wanting me to say Super on the end of .38. But it settled the nerves. I figured whoever was in the SUV was long gone, and if they were someone I should worry about, that worry was doing seventy-five miles an hour down a dark road. I hoped.

I looked back that way. No lights. No shapes in the dark. Just lots of empty pasture. I didn't see any cows. Maybe Bert was planning to go into that business. Or maybe he had been in that business, but no more. Maybe he just liked cows, and that's why he hung out at the auction barn.

I stepped out of the car, put the gun and flashlight in my coat pocket, and pulled on the gloves. I walked up to the front door. A cement block served as a footstep. I stepped up on it, tried to look through the little diamond-shaped glass on the door, but it was designed for looks, not use. It was opaque. It was certainly nice that a fine wood-and-aluminum rectangle like a mobile home had so much class about its door window. Inside, maybe there was a chandelier over a coffee table.

I knocked, lightly at first, and then more briskly. I went around the trailer to the back. There was a rickety, weathered porch there. I went up on it and knocked again. My knock echoed through the trailer and then the noise died like a ball that had quit bouncing. I walked around the trailer and tried to look in the windows, but all the curtains were drawn, and I had to stand on my tiptoes to look at them.

I could hear the air conditioner that poked out of the bedroom window humming, which, considering we were on the edge of winter, seemed unnecessary.

I went to the front door again, thought about trying to jimmy it, but couldn't see any future in that, other than a visit to the Camp Rapture jail.

Then I thought, What the hell, and tried the doorknob.

It was unlocked.

I wasn't sure if that was a good thing or not. I looked at the edge of the door frame, near the lock. The wood was cracked there. It was the kind of thing a professional could do in a second, and almost soundlessly. The hair on the back of my neck stood up like brush bristles.

I opened the door and hoped what I smelled was a rat in the wall, but I had smelled that before and I knew what it was. It wasn't old death. It was the smell of fresh blood and excrement, the common result of violent death.

The thing to do was to call the police and not go inside. So I didn't call them and went inside. That was my style. I put my right hand in my coat pocket to keep the gun warm, and used my other to flash the light around, but otherwise, I stayed where I was, sniffing that stink, half-expecting someone to pop out at me.

There was a very large and nice television in the front room, and it took up most of it. There was a painting of dogs on the wall playing poker. Someone had to have one. I spent more time admiring it than it deserved. The place was so small, living there might require acrobatics. I kept looking at that painting of the dogs playing poker in the light of my flash. Anything to keep me from going back there where the stench was coming from. The air conditioner hummed and it was cold enough to be uncomfortable.

Finally, I pulled my feet loose and started walking. There was a bedroom in the rear of the trailer, and the door to it was open. I went inside. I bounced the light around. It looked as if it had been hit by a small tornado. Drawers were emptied on the floor, on the bed. Under some of the stuff on the bed was a heap that seemed to be the source of the smell.

Since no vampires seemed to be lurking in the shadows, I put the gun in my pocket and took out my flash and turned it on, shined it on the bed. I took hold of the edge of the covers topping the heap and moved them.

A body was underneath, not sleeping. I pulled my T-shirt up over my nose, but it didn't help much; that blood and excrement smell was stout. The body lay on its back and it was nude and dark and bloody. I moved the flash over it carefully.

It was, as I expected, Bert.

There was a hole in the forehead. The bedsheets behind the head were thick with dark, drying blood. In the beam of my light it looked as if the victim had leaked black wax. His hands were stretched out and held with rope. The rope had been pulled down on both sides of the bed and tied to the bed rail. His feet were tied off at the end of the bed in the same way.

I moved the beam down his bare chest, down to the groin. There was something there that looked like the remains of a penis, because it had been worked over with something sharp. You might call it a major circumcision.

A cockroach crawled out from under the body and scuttled over the sheet, proving Bert wasn't much of a housekeeper or the killers had brought their own roaches. Between his legs, about calf level, there was a design drawn on the sheets in dried blood.

A devil's head.

25

I threw up out by the car because the stench of the dead man was still in my nostrils. It wasn't the first time I had seen anyone dead or smelled death, but tonight it clung to me like shit on a stick.

Driving home, I could still smell it.

Several times I thought about pulling out my cell and dialing the cops, or calling Leonard, or Marvin, telling them what I found, but I didn't. I don't know why. I was overwhelmed with the feeling that had I arrived at the trailer just a little bit earlier, I could have ended up like Bert. It wasn't my first close call, but it seemed to me there had been a bunch of them now, and that my string was bound to be running out.

As I went along the road that led out to the main highway, I kept feeling as if I were disconnected. A part of me kept wondering if I was still asleep, dreaming about all this. But I knew better.

When I got to the highway, I saw a dark SUV pull out and move up quickly. Maybe it was the one I had seen before. Maybe not.

I put my foot on it and sped up. I might as well have been walking. The SUV passed me like I was standing still, but when it got in front of me, it kept going.

Moving along like a jet. Pretty soon, it was out of sight.

My cell rang. I almost crawled out of my skin when it did.

It was Bert's number.

I said, "Hello."

The phone went dead.

Shit. They had Bert's phone, and they had my number. If they had a way of tracing it, they could find me, and these days, with all the Internet stuff, that would be easy. I didn't like it. I didn't like what I did for a living. I didn't like me. I didn't like most anything I could think of at that moment.

I thought about Bert, and I thought about a person, or persons, who could do to him what they had. He'd been tortured. Maybe he did know something important, or maybe it was back to what I had thought before, they thought he did. Now maybe they thought I knew something.

Damn.

When I got home, I got out of the car and went carefully inside with my gun drawn. I looked around, went upstairs, looked it over.

I went back downstairs and looked out the living room windows, and then the kitchen windows, but didn't see anything that made me want to start shooting. I felt strangely weak, in a way I had never felt before.

I thought about Brett. I could call her. I could tell her what I found.

I didn't.

I sat in a chair in the living room and laid the automatic on the chair arm. I kept telling myself to get up and go to bed or make a call to someone. Leonard. Marvin. Brett. But I didn't move.

I didn't want to go upstairs.

I didn't want anyone sneaking up on me.

I wanted to be near the front and rear doors by being in the center of the living room in the chair. I tried to sleep in the chair, but I couldn't. I felt like I wanted to go to the bathroom, but I couldn't.

I sat there.

And sat there, and then I realized I had gone to the bathroom. I was in the chair and I hadn't got up, and I could smell myself. My mind seemed rational. Like it knew what was going on, but it wouldn't connect to the physical. My emotions were on holiday.

Time folded in on itself. I didn't move. I sat there and smelled myself and thought about getting up, but still I sat.

I had a feeling vampires were in the room. That they had turned to shadow and slid under the door and were behind me, but I couldn't turn to look. I couldn't move. I felt them come closer and closer and closer. They were crawling along the walls. I could see them out of the corner of my eye. When cars drove by on the road out front their headlights moved the vampires away and washed them into the walls, and as the lights passed, the vampires returned and melted down the walls and into the floor. I sensed they were flowing along close to my feet.

But still, I sat.

The sun came up. It reddened the curtains.

The day passed in what seemed like instants. I watched shadows moving along the wall again. They weren't vampires this time. They were glimpses of time being stolen from my life. The room was as dark and heavy as if it were covered in thick black velvet.

I heard the door open, and Brett called out, "Hap?"

I tried to answer, but all my answers, like my emotions, were still on vacation. I kept thinking I would gather them up and weld them together and be myself, but I didn't move. I might as well have been a turnip waiting to be plucked.

The room grew suddenly bright.

Brett touched me and called my name, and then I saw her nose wrinkle up from the smell of me, and I wanted to say I was sorry, but it just wouldn't come out. Then I climbed into my spaceship and stretched out on my bunk and buckled in and looked through the windshield at the stars and colorful planets moving closer. I was cruising through the great black star-studded forever that was space. Twinkle, twinkle, little star, vampires suck blood, and humans make war. Ducks have feathers, goats have hair, pigs have pink feet, and Davy Crockett killed a bear.

A big black planet swung in from the right, and I could see the planet had eyes. The planet moved closer and I could see the planet had a resemblance to Leonard. The planet Leonard had arrived, and the knowledge of that made me feel better.

I heard Brett say, "I found him like this. I checked his vitals. They seem okay. Maybe I should have called nine-one-one."

"I got him," Leonard said.

I wanted to say something back. I could hear them and I could understand their words, but what they said were like trains passing in the night. I could see their words go by, but no way they were gonna stop and let me ride.

I was pulled right out of my spaceship. I felt myself floating upward (antigravity, baby), and I could see Leonard's face clearly, and he was looking right at me. Brett said, "I'll call the doctor."

"He don't need no doctor," Leonard said.

"But—"

"I got him. Open the bathroom door."

Yeah. That would be nice. I need to go to the bathroom. Again.

And then I was sitting on the floor by the tub and Leonard was leaning over the tub running water. I finally turned my head. It was no more trouble than trying to screw a large bolt through the center of the earth.

"Throw this shit away," Leonard said.

I saw Brett's hands taking my old clothes.

I felt cold. And then I was lifted, and I felt wet. But it was a warm wet. I didn't feel cold anymore. I was drifting comfortably through space, and the great black planet called Leonard was leaning over me in the tub.

"He going to be okay?" Brett said.

"Goddamn right he is."

I closed my eyes, and as I drifted down into the wet warmth, I heard Brett say, "What . . . what is it? What's wrong?"

"Life," Leonard said.

26

When I opened my eyes I was still warm, but I wasn't wet. I was warm because I was in bed with the covers pulled up to my chest. Leonard was sitting by my bedside reading one of my paperbacks. I said, "What are you doing here?"

"Well," Leonard said. "I finish this book, I'm gonna steal everything you got while you're lying there like a dumb ass. And then I'm gonna turn heterosexual and me and Brett are gonna run off together, but not until we sell your organs to science and burn the house down and collect the insurance money. I was thinking we might buy a pig to take with us, start a hog farm."

"You need two pigs," I said. "One male, one female."

"Guess I hadn't thought that through." Leonard reached out and took my hand. "You back, brother?"

"Was I gone?"

"Oh yeah."

"Brett? I remember seeing her, hearing her, but I couldn't answer. Where is she?"

"Downstairs fixing me and her some breakfast. Want me to add you to the list?"

"That would be nice . . . But, what happened?"

"You had what some people call a nervous breakdown, and what I call a major fuckup by way of an easy chair and crapping your pants. You peed too. The world got hold of you and whipped your ass, Hap. But only for a round. You're back now and pretty soon you'll be off the stool and back in the fight. Though you may have to start with some tomato cans and work your way up to the contenders."

"I'm glad Brett called you."

"I'm not. I had to change your clothes and bathe you, wash the shit off, and then dry your ass with a towel, put you in your jammies, and carry you upstairs. I tell you now, boy, you got to lay off the pancakes if you want me carryin' your fat ass up a flight of stairs. Let me have Brett fix you some eggs or somethin'."

Leonard got up and walked toward the bedroom door.

I said, "Leonard."

He paused, looked at me. "Yeah?"

"A man couldn't ask for a better brother."

"Hell, I know that."

27

I was halfway through my scrambled eggs and bacon, sitting in bed with a tray, enjoying it, looking forward to my coffee, when suddenly I felt there was something I was trying to remember, something I wanted to say. It roamed around the alleys of my mind like a drunk trying to find where he'd dropped his car keys.

Brett was in bed with me, stretched out beside me, a pillow propped behind her head. She wore shorts and a sweatshirt. She smelled like perfume and fried foods. Leonard was in the chair next to the bed. He had been talking about things that didn't matter, and it was exactly what I wanted to hear. Those things that didn't matter were really good conversation right then. I knew Leonard thought I was bad off because he even asked me if I would tell a joke. He hates my jokes.

I didn't have a joke. I was too weak to have a joke. I could see he was actually relieved, and so was Brett.

"Did Leonard tell you I wanted to put you down, but he insisted you were going to be all right? I was about to call the vet and have it done, and he showed up."

"There was a moment there when I would have invited it."

She pushed my hair off my forehead and kissed my cheek.

Right then I loved her more than I had ever loved her.

I was sipping on my coffee when I had a flash as clear as daylight. I said, "Bert's dead."

"Bert?" Brett said.

"Mini's stepfather," Leonard said.

"He's dead," I said.

"You just have a psychic vision or something?" Leonard asked.

I put my cup of coffee on the tray. "No," I said. "I saw him dead. Last night."

I told them what I had seen.

Leonard said, "Maybe you never left the chair. Maybe you thought you saw what you saw. You told me vampires were after you."

"I did?"

"You did."

"It all seems like a dream. I think I remember thinking I'd call the police, then Marvin, then you, Leonard."

"Was I on the list?" Brett asked.

"You were next."

"But you didn't call," Leonard said.

"I guess not."

"It was a kind of trigger, Hap, you seeing Bert's body, or thinking you did, or dreaming you did. It was the straw that broke the camel's back. And in case you're not following my cliché, you're the camel."

"You really think you saw a dead man?" Brett said. "Or are you screwed in the head, honey?"

"Sympathy like that," Leonard said, "is why you're a nurse."

"I'm just sayin'," Brett said.

"I don't know," I said. "I really don't. I'd have a hard time trying to remember my shoe size right now. But it seemed real. I had this feeling that things weren't right, and I went out there. He called, see, and I went to sleep, and I woke up feeling like it wasn't right."

"But you don't know for a fact you went to see him?" Brett said.

I shook my head.

"You been kind of goofy lately," Leonard said. "I saw this coming, but I wasn't expecting it to be like this."

"What were you expectin'?" I asked.

"It didn't involve you shittin' yourself while sittin' in a big armchair," Leonard said. "That much I can tell you."

"Which, by the way," Brett said, "I have disposed of the chair. I took it to the dump. You owe me a chair, Hap."

"I'll get right on that," I said.

Leonard got up and started for the door.

I said, "Where are you goin'?"

"To get Bert's Camp Rapture address from the folder, then I'm going to go see if you're nuts."

28

Sometime later, Leonard came through the bedroom door. Brett and I were snuggled up together under the covers.

"Glad I didn't come back fifteen minutes later," Leonard said. "Or was it fifteen minutes earlier?"

"Whatever time you came in, it would have been the same situation," Brett said. "His little friend is as tired as he is."

I said, "Do we need to get me sized for a straitjacket?"

"It was just like you said, including the devil drawing on the sheets. The place was thrown about, maybe just to look like a robbery. He was tortured good. His tongue was cut out. Air conditioner was running, which might have muffled screams and it would keep the body from going to rot too fast. That happened, you could smell that stink for a mile. And maybe Bert just liked it cold. Bottom line, though, is he's dead."

"Jesus," Brett said.

"Good to know I'm not going to be spending Christmas in a rubber room. But, on the other hand, bad to know Bert really is dead."

"Yeah, with his passing, the world has really lost a big bit of charm. As for you, you're not off the nut hook yet. I think you need to stay where you are for a while. Get your marbles back together."

"Yeah, you're kind of fucked up," Brett said. "You boys want more coffee?"

"That would be nice," Leonard said.

"Well," Brett said, "I want some too, so I'm going to do what any good domesticated woman does, I'm going to have Leonard make it."

"Hell with that," Leonard said. "I'm going to the coffee shop."

"You know what?" Brett said. "I think I was just bitten by a ghost of women past. I'll go down and make the coffee. You two visit."

When Brett was downstairs, Leonard pulled his chair closer to me. "You feelin' better, brother?"

"I think so. I'm just not entirely certain what's real and what isn't, but more and more things are coming back to me."

"Do you remember that five hundred dollars you owe me?"

"Nope. That isn't coming back."

Leonard grinned and gave my hand a pat. He said, "Now, while you're weak, I can smother you with a pillow."

"Way I feel, you could smother me with a thought."

We sat silent for a few moments.

"Sometimes in war," Leonard said, "there are soldiers who killed too much and saw too much, and they have nervous collapses. Sometimes they have it right there, right after they killed someone, or lost a buddy, but mostly they come home and have it years later."

"And you never had any of that?"

"Once I woke up in a sweat remembering that I had lost a harmonica in the war."

"A harmonica?"

"My uncle gave it to me, and I had it over there. I never played it. He gave it to me when I was a kid. That and a cap gun and cowboy bandanna. I lost the cap gun, and once when I was in the woods, hunting, and had to shit, I wiped my ass on the bandanna and lost my sentimentality toward it. But I had that harmonica, and though I couldn't play a lick, I took it to war with me. It was kind of like a charm."

"So, you're telling me I lost my harmonica and had a nervous breakdown? I don't own a harmonica, Leonard."

"In a way, I am telling you that you lost your harmonica. There were guys went over there to war and came back and went along fine for years. I was once told by an army buddy that anyone killed someone had some kind of hole in them, even if they felt the person killed needed to be killed. Because on some level, human beings identify with other human beings to such an extent they start to see themselves as the dead human. You may be okay for a while, but in time, those things you do, things you've seen, they come home to roost, like pterodactyls."

"Do you have moments like that?" I asked.

"I don't. Not if I thought what I did was the right thing to do. I'm pretty self-righteous. I mean, there are guys out there, sociopaths that end up in war, and for them it's like a free hand job every day. They like it. They don't feel. That's different. I think it needs to be done, I don't brood. You, you're always digging into your feelings. You leave them raw, mess with them so much. You've seen plenty, but last night you saw one too many. And I think

Vanilla Ride, meeting her, may have been a big trigger, not just poor old Bert. She was the gun. Bert was the bullet."

Vanilla had been a while ago, but he was right, she was in the back of my mind all the time.

"Vanilla is a beautiful woman," Leonard said, "charming, very feminine, and she can kill you with an ice pick or a gun, maybe her bare hands, and sleep like a baby. And I know you. In the back of your mind you're thinking: Once she was a kid like me, and she grew up to kill, and she grew up do it for money and not care who she killed or why. You feel like you might be slipping over into her bit of darkness. I tell you, man, no way. You ain't comin' from, and ain't never been comin' from, the farm where she was raised."

"Farm?"

"Figure of speech."

"How bad was I?" I said.

"I've seen a lot worse. But, know what I think? I think you might have sat in that chair for days, maybe starved to death if Brett hadn't come along, called me." Leonard swallowed and his facial expression changed. "You know what Brett said to me when you were in the chair? She said he's your brother, he loves you, maybe more than me. Fix him."

"And you did," I said.

"I put a Band-Aid on it. You got to be your own doctor. A little bed rest perks you up. A little experience helps you deal with it. But it's like a super staph infection. It gets better, but it doesn't go away."

29

In Marvin's office, he said, "I thought you fuckers had retired."

"No," Leonard said. "We were on strike."

"For what?"

"Better working conditions."

"Well, you're shit out of luck."

"What we figured," Leonard said. "That's why the strike is over."

Marvin eyed me. "You're awful quiet. Usually I can't shut you up. No wisecracks?"

"Not today," I said.

"Hap found a body. Bert, Mini's stepdad. He's been killed."

"No shit," Marvin said.

"I just missed the murderer," I said, and I told him what we knew. About how Bert was scared, and claimed to have information, and then he was dead. I told him about the SUV, the phone call from Bert's phone.

"You tell the police?" Marvin asked.

"Not yet."

"That's not smart," Marvin said.

"I haven't been feeling smart," I said. "I have been, shall we say, under the weather."

"I can work this out a bit," Marvin said. "An anonymous tip. Let the cops know the body is there, but not who told them. Or I know a couple of them well enough they'll pretend they don't know who told them. You all right, Hap?"

"Pretty much," I said.

Marvin picked up a pencil from his desk and tapped his teeth with it. "How does Bert's murder tie in with the rest of it?"

"Therein lies the pickle," Leonard said. "We don't know."

The pickle of it all hung in the air like a zeppelin.

"So we don't know shit?" Marvin asked.

"If we do," Leonard said, "we haven't figured out that we do. Not yet. But no doubt in our minds, it's all connected."

"You said Bert thought someone was after him?" Marvin said. "Couldn't it have been someone else did it? Someone not connected to all this? I mean some reason besides our case?"

"Yeah," I said. "But it's all a little too sweet to be a coincidence. We talk to Bert. He wants to see us. He ends up dead. And I get a call on his phone, and a hang-up. I think that was a kind of threat. A warning at least."

"All right, then," Marvin said. "See if you can tie it all together."

"We will go about detecting, then," Leonard said, standing up.

"You mean you two will go about bumbling in the hopes that happens to lead to something."

"Yeah," Leonard said. "That's pretty much it."

30

Out in the parking lot, as we got in Leonard's car, he said, "To Marvin, we are nothing more than a couple of minions. Carrier pigeons to carry messages and bring messages back. Slaves to his judgment. Faces in the crowd."

"You've had way too much coffee," I said.

"I do feel a little itchy, like my nerves could jerk a decorative knot in my dick. But, minions though we may be, it beats honest work."

"Actually, we don't seem to do much, just find out about dead people," I said.

"And in your case, you even found one that's fresher than the rest."

"He wasn't all that fresh."

"Since the others, the vampires, are all in the ground," Leonard said. "He was the lily of the bunch."

"Ha! If they're vampires, they may not be in the ground."

"Oh, you are wise."

When we were well situated in the car, seat-belted in and hoping it would start, Leonard said, "I'm confused."

"About what?"

"Who do we annoy next? We have a list, but . . . who?"

"I vote Cason Statler," I said.

"Why?"

"Because we can."

"Now you're startin' to sound like yourself," Leonard said.

But I wasn't myself. I wasn't even close.

The drive over to Camp Rapture was nice because it was a pretty day. The rain had cleared up and the sun was out, and the car was a little warm inside. We wheeled to the *Camp Rapture Report,* the newspaper Cason worked for, and went inside.

Cason was sitting at his desk in the middle of the newspaper office. There were other reporters around, but fewer than I had imagined. There was also an advertising department. One of the women who worked there was overweight and frumpy with piss-blonde hair that looked to have been made by electricity and a sense of humor. She was wearing a too-short top that showed a lot of belly and a silver belly ring. She had on shorts that showed way too much ass and on the ass was a tattoo that looked like something an arthritic chicken had scratched in the dirt while dying.

My take is you can dress any way you want, but my amendment to that is that you have to have mirrors at your house, and you have to use them, and you must not lie to yourself about what they show.

"Damn," I said. "I think my right eye just went dead."

"Wishful thinking," Leonard said.

"Oh, the humanity."

Cason looked up from his work, saw us, stopped typing, and watched as we approached his desk. There was one spare chair, and I took it. Leonard put his hip against the side of Cason's desk. All three of us looked at the woman in advertising with the too-little clothes and the too-much flesh.

"I try to forget she's over there," Cason said, "and then I get my mind off forgetting, and look up, and there she is, and I'm wounded all over again."

I said, "Does she actually sell any advertising?"

"She threatens to take the shorts off if they don't buy any," Cason said.

"Ouch," Leonard said.

"She's the curse of the newspaper," Cason said. "The editor is starting a dress code just to get some clothes on her. The flyer went out today from the boss saying we got to dress nicer, and a certain way. Normally I'm against dress codes. I think it violates our civil rights, but in Carrie's case, I'm going to make an exception. You got to think of the children. Small animals. Our way of life. The planet earth."

"If you're through insulting the poor woman," I said, "is there a place where we can talk private?" I said.

"The break room."

Our trip to the break room was short. By the time we had gotten bad coffee in Styrofoam cups and told what we knew to Cason, we were being shuffled away. Cason followed us out to the car. He said, "There's this guy works here, does research, Mercury is his last name, he can find something about anything. I'm gonna put him on this."

"Really?" Leonard said. "His name is Mercury?"

"Really," Cason said. "He lives for research, and anything to do with something odd, that's his meat. Dumb-asses who think they're vampires, that's odd and he'll like it, and he'll research them until he falls over dead. I'll talk to him and see if he can get on it."

"You seem quick to shuffle us off."

"Got a lunch date."

"With a lady?" I said.

"None of your business," he said, got in his car, and drove away.

31

As we were driving, Leonard said, "You think Cason's too busy dropping the rope down the well to do us any good?"

"I think he's the kind of guy that can screw and chew gum and do math problems all at the same time."

"I doubt Cason's date would appreciate his ability to do more than one thing at a time."

"True," I said, "but my guess is he'll have lunch, knock him off a piece, get with this Mercury fella, and have something for us pretty damn quick. He's pretty high-energy."

"And if your description is right, he's not particularly thoughtful," Leonard said.

Leonard made a curve and looked at me out of the corner of his eye.

"How you feelin', Hap?"

"I don't know," I said. "It comes in waves. Sometimes I feel fine, other times I want to go back to that big armchair and not get up."

"The chair's at the dump, and since we're not going to the dump to let you sit in it, that means you just got to live with things."

"How do you do it, Leonard?"

"Because I have to."

"That's no kind of answer."

"It's my answer. I look at it this way. If what I choose to do seems right to me, I do it."

"And what if," I said, "what I choose to do seems right, but isn't. Ku Klux Klan people think they're right, but they aren't."

"I get your point. But you just made a point. You said they aren't right, those KKK fucks, and being a black man, I have to agree. But saying they're wrong means you have what you think is a clear-cut position, and you back it up with experience and facts. Like it or not, you believe you can tell right from wrong, and I trust your judgment and mine on those matters more than I trust the judgment of paranoid and inferior-feeling assholes who are all about making people's lives miserable because they can. I'm simple enough about the matter to consider that if I'm doing something to protect someone or make their life better, and I have the ability to do it, and I'm going to feel good about myself afterward, that's what I do."

"Seems more complicated than that to me," I said.

"Didn't say it wasn't complicated for some. What I said was it's easy for me. Do you think if we hadn't killed those who were trying to kill us in the past, they would have let us go with a pat on the butt? Do you really think there's a god that sorts them out and punishes them if someone here in reality land doesn't?"

"No. But we're part of the problem."

"Let me ask you why we put ourselves in those positions."

"We're stupid."

"Next answer."

I sighed. "We were trying to help someone, or we were trying to help ourselves, and at least once, we were trying to make some money."

Leonard turned a wicked eye toward me, and then put it back on the road.

"That was my fault," I said.

"Just looking for an acknowledgment . . . Let me give you the bottom line, Hap. People we've chosen to help over the years, had we not helped them, it wouldn't have turned out well. The people we killed, if we hadn't, would have gone on doing what they were doing, which wasn't good. You are who you are, and you are an avenging angel. You were born to it. For some years I've been trying to figure what my career ought to be. What can I make of myself? Then one night, while I was pulling my johnson, having to use both hands, of course, I had a epiphany. I'm following my calling as surely as those who grow up to be astronauts or firemen or doctors. So are you. Maybe it's a kind of post-traumatic stress you're suffering. But I don't think the reason you had a nervous breakdown was about what you've done. It's about you trying to find a way to stop being you, and you can't."

32

We went to my house and sat around because we weren't exactly sure what in the hell we were doing or how to go about it.

Brett was at work, wouldn't be home until midnight, so we broke out the checkers and played for a while.

Late afternoon my cell rang. It was Cason.

"Mercury is on it, and he'll have something for us day after tomorrow at the latest, maybe sooner."

"Us?"

"Am I helping, or what?"

"You are."

"Then it's us. So long, Hap."

. . .

We were too lazy to cook, so we drove into town and had dinner at a café. We digested awhile at a coffee shop, then went over to the gym to work out, kick the bag and punch the mitts, then we drove back. As we turned on my street, we saw a car stop three houses up from mine in the Apostle's Baptist Church parking lot and turn off the lights. The car was one of those low-slung jobs that in the light from the street looked like an angry rodent crouched to attack.

Leonard slowed, said, "Think maybe those are eager church-goers who have come to wait until the church doors open on Sunday?"

"Seems unlikely."

"My thoughts exactly."

We drove by. I turned in the seat and looked out the back. The car was still sitting there. A little red dot from a cigarette was visible. No one had got out.

"What do you think?" I said.

"I think they're bracing themselves to do something bad, and I got a feeling it isn't the church they got a quarrel with."

"Couldn't be us, could it?" I said.

"It's hard to believe anyone could be angry with us," Leonard said, "but yes, I believe they have come to visit us. Call it instinct. Call it experience."

"Someone somewhere is always mad at us."

"Yeah, that's probably more accurate."

Leonard turned the corner and we went around the block and on the back street. We parked at the curb next to an empty lot with high grass. I opened Leonard's glove box and got out his automatic.

"That's my gun."

"Not today," I said.

Leonard pulled a short club out from under his car seat, lifted his deerstalker from the middle of the seat, and put it on. We got out and went across the field. At the end of the field we came to a backyard, and crossed that without any dogs barking. From there we could see mine and Brett's house and the board fence around the backyard.

We didn't say anything to each other. Sliding across the yard, through the night, we came to the fence and climbed over it, and fell into the backyard. We went across the dead grass and I got my key and opened the back door and we slipped in.

I went right, toward the kitchen, and Leonard turned to the left, toward the downstairs closet.

I was at the corner of the kitchen and the living room, thinking maybe we were overreacting, and that the car we'd seen had been nothing more than the preacher of the church stopping by to pick up a Bible, when the front door was kicked open with a bang and two men with guns plunged inside along with the light from the street lamp.

33

It was as I feared and suspected. Our beatings hadn't put the fear of the devil into them after all. They had found out who we were and where we were, but as luck would have it, they didn't know what car we were driving or that we had passed them by on the street.

The first one in the door was Thomas. He had a cast on his right hand. It was up in a sling. The other was Chunk, and he was limping, had a cast on his leg and some kind of heel on it to help him walk. They both had handguns.

Without meaning to, I said aloud:

"Really? You've got broken hands and legs, and . . . Shit, really?"

Thomas and Chunk paused there in the light, as if for a dance number. Thomas saw my shape and lifted the gun, held it sideways like a movie thug, said, "You fucks broke my right hand, mother-fucker. But I'm left-handed."

There was a *ca-chunk* sound, and then I heard Leonard in the shadows by the open closet say, "Yeah, and I got me a shotgun in the gauge of twelve from the closet, cocksucker."

The world seemed stuck in amber.

Finally, Thomas said, "Well, okay."

That hung in the air like a popcorn fart for about thirty seconds.

Thomas's gun was still pointed in my direction. I had Leonard's automatic held down by my side. I said, "Put the gun down, or Leonard will blow you both out the door like so much dust."

"Actually," Leonard said, "what I've found, you shoot a guy with a shotgun, he don't blow backwards so much as he drops like a curtain and it makes a mess you wouldn't believe. There ain't enough janitors in town to clean it up right, but then again, that's just my personal experience."

As he said this, Leonard was moving forward, the shotgun at his shoulder.

"You know, I got a gun too," I said. "I could shoot somebody."

They ignored me. They were all about that shotgun.

Besides, I had yet to lift the automatic from my side. My face was covered in sweat and my gun hand was trembling. I had tunnel vision. You get that when you're scared. It's a thing happens when you're in a tight situation, especially one of potential violence. Me, I had gotten over it a long time ago. I could control it.

Or could. But tonight, not so much.

Leonard hit a light switch.

Thomas, without lowering the gun he was pointing at me, glanced at Leonard, did a kind of double take at the hat.

"You don't worry about it," Leonard said. "How's it gonna be? A maybe shot you get to take at me and Hap, or a certain boom from the shotgun, and the both of you blood and rags. My aim don't have to be as good as yours."

Thomas and Chunk let their handguns drift to their sides.

"Ain't nobody doin' nothing," Chunk said. "I told this fool we ought not mess with you two crazies."

Thomas turned his head slightly, looked at Chunk. Right then he knew his number one man had climbed out the window, so to speak.

"Now, with your guns at your side," I said, "dip your knees . . . Oh, sorry, Chunk. How about just drop them."

"You two," Thomas said, "I hate you both. I hate you cocksuckers big-time."

"That comes up a lot," Leonard said.

34

The cops came and took Thomas and Chunk. Drake, the chief of police, was with them. He was lean and black and his nose looked even flatter than when I had seen him last. He stayed after the other cops left. We had the lights on now. Very cheery.

Leonard moved the shotgun so he could sit on the couch. Drake said, "Don't handle the gun anymore."

I sat in a stuffed armchair and tried not to let anyone see that my hands were shaking. They had been that way for days, and tonight, after the events, they were shaking even more. I shoved them down by my sides in the chair.

"I'll take that with me when I leave," Drake said, nodding at the gun.

"Okay," Leonard said.

They had already taken the automatic, which was registered to Leonard. I was a little uncertain how that would play out, but I didn't point out it wasn't mine or that I was the one that had held it. I also didn't mention that we had a number of cold pieces hidden around the house, the best of them upstairs in the crawl space above the closet.

Drake declined me fixing him a cup of coffee, giving him a soda, anything. No bribes were considered. He sat on the couch and shook his head a few times. It made me feel sort of sorry for him, and sad about the two of us.

"They did break in," I said.

"Yes," Drake said. "That's why they are gone and you are still here. But, you know, what they told me was you two broke into their house and broke them up a few days ago, and they were paying you back."

"That's some story," I said.

"Yeah," Leonard said. "That's some shit, that is."

"You did break them up, didn't you?"

"I'm trying to remember," I said.

"Never mind," Drake said. "Not right now. I don't want to hear the lies. It just makes me tired."

There was a knock on the door. Leonard answered. It wasn't anyone else there to kill us. It was Marvin. Of course, considering the circumstances, maybe he wanted to kill us too.

Drake, still sitting on the couch, looked up at Marvin, said, "You got to get you some better friends."

"Tell me about it," Marvin said.

He took a chair across the way and sat. He and Drake looked at each other like two parents who knew how bad their kids were and had both had just about enough of it. Reform school seemed to be in mine and Leonard's offing.

"We didn't shoot anyone," I said.

"No," Drake said. "You didn't do that."

"I wanted to," Leonard said, "real bad. But I held back. I fought against that bad side and done good. That ought to amount to something."

I was thinking that if it hadn't been for Leonard I would have been dead. I had frozen. I had been unable to move. My brain went blank and my hands had felt like catcher's mitts, too big and clumsy to use. The thought of aiming a gun at someone again, pulling the trigger, I hadn't been able to do it. I wondered if I'd ever be able to do it. I was trying to decide if that was a good thing.

If Leonard hadn't been there, one thing was certain, at that moment in time, good it would not have been. Right now a crew with tweezers would be extracting my brain matter from the wall.

Drake said, "So, you boys didn't do anything to piss anyone off? I find that hard to believe. You always piss me off."

"Let me give you a scenario," Marvin said. "Say there was this little old lady, and she was walking home from the grocery, and this guy, we'll call him Thomas, assaulted her for the money in her change purse, and that money was less than a hundred dollars. And there were people in the neighborhood who saw this happen, and I know them, and they told me it happened, but they wouldn't go on record, wouldn't talk to the police, even though the little old lady, we'll call her Mrs. Johnson, because that's her name, talked to the police and told them, but there was no validation, no proof. At least not anything the cops could use."

"Let me finish this for you," Drake said. "But the little old lady told you and you got these two guys to go over and politely ask them for the money."

"Very politely," Marvin said.

"And things got testy, and they decided to hurt your two boys, and your two boys hurt them instead. So the other boys had a grudge against your boys, found out where Hap lived. So Hap and Leonard, innocent and as pure as baby chicks, are attacked in Hap's home."

"That's pretty much it," Marvin said.

"Yeah," Leonard said. "That sounds about right."

"Is that mostly true?" Drake asked Marvin.

"Yep," Marvin said. "Mostly."

"Did the little old lady get her money back?"

"Yep."

Drake nodded. "Well, I don't know. Maybe I can play it some kind of way where the two numbnuts—the other two numbnuts—go down for breaking and entering. They'll tell their story to a lawyer, but even if it's a true story they tell, there's still the part that involves guns and breaking into a home. But the story Marvin just told me, supported somewhat by our two friends trussed up in plaster casts, sort of supports you two breaking into their home."

"Oh," I said.

"Anyone see it happen?" Drake asked. "This event involving you two that didn't happen, but might have."

"If it happened," I said, "and I'm not saying it did. I don't think so."

"And in this case," Marvin said, "these two citizens called the police and asked for assistance. Those two goobers didn't call anyone, so their story is well after the fact and could just be a goddamn lie. This could have been nothing more than home invasion. Possible robbery. Right?"

"Yeah," Leonard said. "We could have killed them and buried them in the backyard and not mentioned it. Planted some flowers over them. But we called, because that's just the kind of guys we are. Fucking law-abiding citizens."

"Satisfied?" Marvin asked.

"No," Drake said. "Not really. But I think I can live with it. I can't promise they can't stir enough shit that charges get brought against the stooges here, but maybe I can get the charges against them trimmed slightly, making them more jovial than they might be otherwise. And maybe part of the persuasion would be they leave you two alone legally."

"How trimmed will their charges be?" Leonard asked.

"They're going to go up for sure. Just can't tell you how long. And you guys, well, if there are no witnesses to fit their story, it's just a story. You two were smart and called the cops. They had guns, you were home, and you had a bigger gun, which is called home protection and self-defense, and nobody was killed."

"That's the story I like," Leonard said. "It has a nice ring to it.

One more thing, if they are mad at us for something they think we did, then they might think the old lady who got robbed ought to get some mojo. She ought to be checked on."

"The two dumb-asses . . . The other two dumb-asses . . . told us you seemed to think you were avenging an old lady you claimed they hurt, and they gave us her name, and we called and checked on her, and she's all right. Of course, if you didn't do what they say you did, then you shouldn't know Mrs. Johnson and what happened to her. Right?"

"Oh, no," Leonard said. "We could know. Word gets around. We heard rumors."

"Rumors?"

"Yep," Leonard said. "Rumors."

Drake kept looking at Leonard out of the corner of his eye. Finally he sat up straight on the couch, looked right at him, said, "Hey, Leonard. I've been trying to kind of let it go. But what in the living hell have you got on your head?"

35

Brett was sitting in the living room with me and Leonard and Marvin. Drake had gone away. It was after midnight and she was back from work. We told her what happened. My first thought was she'd finally decide it was time to ditch me. I was like a shit magnet. It always found me. No matter where I went, what I did, it came flying out of the air and landed on me.

Well, maybe there were things I did that attracted it.

Like breaking that guy's knee, messing up his ribs.

But it wouldn't matter. I could stay home in front of the TV and trouble would arrive in the form of a singing telegram. And if it didn't find me, it would find Leonard, and that was the same as finding me.

"So, you were just minding your own business," Brett said.

"Really," Leonard said. "We were."

"I believe you," she said. "I'm on your side."

"We're the three musketeers," I said. "Oh," I said, looking at Marvin, "sorry to leave you out of the musketeer thing. In the book, there were actually four."

"I don't want to be a musketeer," Marvin said.

"Now, come on," Leonard said. "He didn't mean to hurt your feelings. You can be a musketeer too."

"I'm fine," Marvin said.

"My sense of things," Leonard said, "is that you really do want to be one, and just won't admit it."

"Actually," Brett said, "I always wanted to be a Mouseketeer."

"Oh, Christ," I said, "is there any way some night I can get you to wear a set of mouse ears when we, you know—"

"Oh, hell yeah," Brett said.

Brett went into the kitchen, came back with some corn chips and sodas, said, "Enjoy, this may be as housewifey as I get."

We had at the chips and drinks. It was like a feeding frenzy at the zoo.

"So, the deal is," Brett said, "you're trying to find the connection between the vampires and the man in the trailer, Mini's stepdad? And you're thinking Mini's money is part of the deal?"

"It makes sense," Marvin said. "And I can tell Hap has kept our confidential rule and not mentioned any of this to you."

"Oh, he never shuts up," Brett said.

"Figured as much," Marvin said.

"Want to hear what I think?"

"Might as well."

"Maybe I should wear Leonard's deerstalker since I'm giving my valued investigative opinion based on nothing but a hunch."

Leonard handed it to her and she put it on.

"Whoa," Marvin said. "That looks good on you."

"Hell, yeah," I said. "Forget the mouse ears."

"It looks all right," Leonard said.

"The money is all coincidence," Brett said. "It's clouding your judgment. The law got Godzilla for the murder of that frat boy, but Mini, she got off the hook, and so did the others. They got their wrists slapped. Somewhere, someone's bound to be mad about that, and it doesn't have to do with them being vampires, or there being money involved, or even Ted Christopher being killed. With me so far?"

"We're listening," Marvin said.

"Wouldn't you be mad someone killed someone you loved, and the batch of them got off by tattling?" Brett said.

"They got off because they turned evidence on Godzilla, who did the actual killing," Marvin said. "She was the one stabbed the kid, sucked his blood. I'm not saying they're pure as the driven snow, but they didn't do the stabbing."

"I know," Brett said, "but if someone killed Hap, I wouldn't be satisfied if the one person most responsible went to jail and didn't even get the death penalty. That deal would suck, especially since the others got to go free and weren't even told their breath stinks. If I was the frat boy's family, maybe I would have a serious grudge. Now that I think about it, I've never heard any of you even mention the dead boy's name."

We looked at one another.

"I guess we been thinking it had more to do with Godzilla or Mini or Ted," I said.

"You got your notes, Hap?" Marvin asked.

I got them.

Marvin opened them. "Kid's name was Jason Kincaid. His parents are divorced, and the mother is dead. Cancer. The father is a sixty-year-old accountant in Houston. Had one other child, a girl, Florence, died of a drug overdose. Has some wealthy clients, and therefore is pretty wealthy himself. His name is Howard Kincaid. He was looked at by the cops some years ago. They came up with zip. He hasn't been high on our list, because they caught the one who killed his kid. Godzilla."

"Maybe Kincaid could get another look," I said.

"It's worth a shot," Marvin said. "I could send you boys to meet him, or we could get someone good."

"That is some amusing shit you got going there," Leonard said. "That is funny, how you cut us down, and may really mean it."

Marvin grinned. "I suggest we talk to Cason Statler. He's friends with Mrs. Christopher, and he used to work in Houston. Probably has some contacts you could talk to. And, of course, you can talk to the kid's father. Personally, I don't think there's anything to it—no offense, Brett—as it's been looked into. I'd think the cops would have sensed something being there, even if they are the worst cops since Keystone. But they didn't note a thing. I think it has to do with Mini. I think she's the key, and I think it maybe has to do with Ted. The others are connected, of course, but I think the chain starts with her and has to do with something she or Ted knew or something they did. I think Godzilla may just be unlucky, and that Mom was a bad driver and a drunk. But Kincaid, I don't see it."

"I like my idea," Brett said, "because it's mine."

"May I have my hat back now?" Leonard said.

Brett gave him the hat.

"Jim Bob is from the Houston area," I said. We know him. We've worked with him. Maybe he'd do better than Cason."

"We'd have to pay him out of our money," Marvin said.

No one said anything for a moment. Then Leonard said, "Yeah, you're right, let's get Cason, and we can work on his loyalty to Mrs. Christopher, and just have to buy him lunch or somethin'."

36

After Leonard and Marvin left, I set the door back in place, but it was beyond fixing. I didn't have any boards to nail over it, so I put a chair under the doorknob. A kitten with anger issues could probably have pushed it over, but it was something.

Me and Brett locked ourselves in the upstairs bedroom just in case our two cast-wearing vigilantes escaped the long arm of the law and came after us.

I said, "What you said about the father, Kincaid, that was solid thinking, baby. We've been so certain it was someone who just hated these people for their weirdness, or was one of them, that it didn't occur to us. We should have considered it, but we didn't, and that's why Leonard and I do odd jobs and are not professors of physics."

"That's the truth," Brett said.

"I give you a compliment, and you wound me? You are one mean woman."

"What about Marvin?"

"Well," I said, "I'm not saying you're definitively right and he's wrong, but he thinks of himself as a detective, and on some level, having been a cop, I think he wants to generally believe they know what they're talking about. And usually, truth is, they do. But sometimes, a person standing back from it all can point out the obvious."

She snuggled close. "What made me think of the father, Kincaid, really wasn't obvious thinking."

"No?"

"No. It was those two jackasses that broke into our house. Here are two guys that had their hand, a knee, and a rib broke. A couple of bully types, the sort they always tell you if you stand up to them they won't fight back. But they did."

"Most of those little schoolyard homilies prove to be false. Bullies are not always cowards, but they are always bullies," I said. "And they had guns. That helps make you braver, just in case you're lacking in the courage department."

"They went to the trouble of figuring out who you two were, and coming here. They wanted revenge. I thought Kincaid might feel the same way. And it turns out he has the money to make it happen."

"It was good thinking," I said. "I was thinking the law got Godzilla, so what's for Kincaid to do? It was taken care of. But it wasn't my son. Had it been, I might not be so easily satisfied."

"I'm going to change the subject."

"Okay."

She ran her hand down my side. "Want to make love?"

"Of course," I said. "I'm no idiot."

"No mouse ears and Leonard took his hat back."

"We'll just pretend."

"I can squeak like a mouse."

"Baby, you say the sweetest things."

We made love and fell into an uneasy sleep. Or at least my sleep was uneasy. Within seconds, Brett was sawing logs. Me, I lay there for a while and wondered what would have happened had Leonard not been there with me tonight.

The answer was obvious.

37

Next morning, early, I went to a hardware store and bought the stuff I needed and brought it home. Brett and I replaced the door-jamb and lock, with her doing the precision work. Stuff like that for me is like trying to write cursive on a notepad with my toes while taking verbal directions from a monkey. But with us working together, it was a fair job. It still needed painting, and I had forgotten the paint.

After Brett left for an afternoon shift, I called Leonard, invited him over for lunch. He passed, said he was having lunch with Cason.

I tucked a sandwich away, went to town, and bought some paint. When I got back, Leonard's car was parked in the drive. He had let himself in and was watching the downstairs television, some show about the life of Willie Nelson. Leonard was a bear for all things related to country music.

While I painted the doorjamb and he lounged, I asked him: "What about Cason?"

"He's in. A couple of tacos and I had him on the job."

"When do we go?"

"He's waiting on a call."

Cason had us meet him at the newspaper office, and then took us downstairs to meet Mercury, the man who collected facts. He told us Mercury had been with the paper a long time, and all he did was fact-check and catalog the morgue. He was seldom seen, and his work was rarely questioned. In fact, Cason told us that unless you needed something from downstairs, in what he called the dungeon, you stayed out of there. Mercury liked it that way.

Downstairs was like a hole in the floor with steps and it was crowded with more crap than a junkyard: boxes and files and desks and tables with stacks of papers. It was poorly lit down there.

Mercury had a desk in one corner, and the desk, unlike the rest of the room, was well lit by a gooseneck lamp. He was sitting in front of the desk in a wheeled, wooden chair with his legs crossed. He looked in his thirties, blond hair, blue eyes. A nice-looking guy with a real set of shoulders on him and a face that needed some sun.

He didn't get up as we got closer. We went to him and shook hands.

Cason took a position on the edge of the desk, said, "So, Jack, you find anything?"

"The actual case you're working on, not much. Thing interested me was the devil head at the scene of the murders. I ran it through the computer, and came up with some similar things, but most of it was not similar enough. Except for these."

He turned in his roller chair and picked up the file and spun back around and gave it to me. I opened it. It was a thin file. But there were some crime photos in it. Some may have been suicides, some murders. There were separate photos of little red devil head drawings.

"You got these off the computer?"

"I got some information off the computers, but these photos I got through contacts and through Mrs. Christopher spreading some money around. You can thank her, my government friends, and FedEx for these. The devil head was at the scene of these crimes. Each crime took place miles apart. Let me see the file."

I gave it back to him.

"There was . . . Oh, here's one in Louisiana. Took place not long after the hurricane. The one there was a mobster. The devil head was made really obvious, was drawn on a mirror with the man's blood. The others, they're less obvious. There's Oregon . . . Here's one in New York."

"You're saying these killings have a connection?" Leonard said.

"I'm saying that there's a devil head drawn in blood at these death sites. You want me to do your work for you?"

"That would be nice," I said.

"Here's what I can tell you. Those drawings are either connected, or someone knows about them and copied them for the murders you're investigating. The drawings and the murders, or what look to be suicides—all of them suspicious—took place over five years. There could be more devil heads and more murders that are just not known. Or maybe the killer didn't always do the devil head thing. No one like me has sat down and tracked this stuff, or had the connections to see how many of these devil heads are out there. Me, I like doing this sort of work. You start to see patterns in stuff like this. I'm big on patterns."

"So, is there one person doing all this?" Leonard asked.

"Hell, it could be two, three, a copycat, or a weird coincidence. But it would be one hell of a weird coincidence, and since someone like me would have to put together the fact that there's something to copy, I think a copycat is unlikely as well. Another thing. I checked out any so-called vampire connections to the devil head. Nothing. All of the murders seem unconnected, except for the ones that took place in the East Texas area."

"So what we got is a serial killer?" I said.

Mercury paused. "You know, I'm not so sure. There doesn't seem to be any sexual obsession. There is the devil head, a kind of signature, but maybe our killer just likes to sign his work. It's missing the qualities one usually thinks of when using the term 'serial killer' to mean someone who kills due to some sort of sexual obsession."

"Bert had his tongue cut out," Leonard said. "His penis cut up."

"Torture can be sexual, but I think this was punishment. I think the killers just consider it business. They wanted him to tell them something, and whatever they wanted, he told them. I can promise you that, truth or not."

"Didn't the Son of Sam just shoot people?" I said. "He was a serial killer that didn't mess with the bodies. It was about power. That's what serial killers are really after."

"Yeah," Mercury said. "It could be just like that. I'm not saying I know. I'm saying my experience looking at this kind of stuff for years tells me it may be something else. But, hey, when it comes right down to it, your guess is as good as mine."

38

We went to the hospital and I told Brett we were leaving for Houston. She gave me a kiss and we tried not to make too much of it, me going off only a short time after she had come home, but the feelings were there.

I left her and we drove to my place, and then Leonard's, packed a few overnight things. I saw that Leonard packed the deerstalker. He was swift about it, but I saw it done. At least it was packed and not on his head.

We tooled back to Camp Rapture to get Cason. He had needed time to settle some work details and go home and do his packing.

On the way over, Leonard said, "This is like being in a mystery novel with no detectives."

"Nailed it," I said, and we bumped fists.

We picked up Cason at the address he gave us. It was an apartment complex on the far side of town. Nice place. He told us he had just moved there. We didn't give a shit, but he told us anyway.

Driving along, Cason entertained us with some amusing stories that mostly involved the misfortune of others, which, of course, is what most humor is about, and then explained we would be staying with a friend of his over Houston way, out near the airport. A former police officer.

What he didn't tell us was the former police officer was a hot late-twenties blonde named Constance and she lived in a one-bedroom apartment with a cat named Yo-Yo. She put Leonard and me in the living room, him on the couch, me on a blow-up mattress. We lay there listening to Cason and Constance all night long. For all I knew, maybe Yo-Yo was involved. There was a banging of heads on the bedstead, a whimpering of delight, a cry of servitude, a yelp of triumph, and a smacking of genitals that sounded like someone snapping a leather strap across bucket seats. After a few hours it ceased, then near morning it started up again, loud enough to wake us. Once I thought a siren had gone off, but it was just Constance.

Early morning someone let Yo-Yo out of the bedroom. Listening to that all night, even Yo-Yo's pert little ass made me horny. But Yo-Yo the cat didn't swing that way. To compound matters, it didn't help any that Constance came out of the bedroom adorned in a thin white T-shirt that showed she had very pert nipples and more ass than shirt.

She said excuse me and went to the bathroom and came out wearing dark sweat pants with the T-shirt. The ass was protected, but the nipples still looked like .45 slugs.

Constance offered us some breakfast, and while she was in the kitchen, Cason came out in sweatpants and a wifebeater, scratching his nuts.

I said so Constance couldn't hear, "I had the impression you had a girlfriend at home."

"We aren't connecting like we used to," he said.

"You seem to have been connecting with Constance last night."

"That's none of your business."

"Well, since it sounded like you were screwing next to my air mattress, you made it more of my business than I expected. There were a couple moments when I thought I ought to be wearing some kind of contraceptive. Leonard had morning sickness."

Leonard, who was sitting on the couch in his shorts, nodded. "I'm going out later to buy a bassinet and a baby stroller. Do you have a color preference?"

Cason smiled a smile so thin no teeth were visible, said, "You can both go fuck yourself."

"I've tried," Leonard said. "Doesn't work."

We ate breakfast, and then Cason made some calls on his cell while Constance got ready for work. Turned out she was now working for a private investigation agency. A cooler more successful one than Marvin's. Fifteen agents worked there, and unlike us, they were most likely real detectives, and one of the real detectives was a hot blonde who could screw all night and work all day and had a cat named Yo-Yo.

Constance exited the bathroom, looking professional in a black suit with a frilly white shirt. Her hair was brushed and glossy as a show horse's mane. She sat on the couch and put on her shoes. I noticed her toenails were painted pink and had little silver stars in the middle of them.

I asked her, "Do you know a private investigator from Houston named Jim Bob Luke? Know it's a long shot, but I was just wondering."

"That conceited asshole," she said, giving me a hard look. "Yeah, I know him. He a friend of yours?"

"No," I said. "Leonard knows him."

39

Cason, with his boyish phone charm, got us a meeting with Howard Kincaid.

Driving over there, me at the wheel, I said to Cason, "No problem with him talking with us?"

"I told him we were investigating his son's death, looking for new connections. I didn't have to say much else."

Howard Kincaid had his office in one of the supertall buildings downtown. It seemed to be made completely of glass and metal and the only stone about it was the wide steps in front, and that stone was polished. In the sunlight the building was as shiny as the snot under a kid's nose. There were people moving about on the street and cars crowding mine as I drove. I was glad I was visiting Houston, not living there. Three days in a place like this I might have a screaming fit. Of course, that couldn't be any worse than sitting in a chair and crapping on myself.

We found a parking place in an underground garage and took an elevator up to the floor we wanted. When the elevator opened, the floor was so freshly buffed it gave off a shimmer like a heat wave in the desert, not quite as bright as the building outside, but bright enough. There was a large opening at one end of the hall, and in it were a lot of plants. It also had brightly colored birds in cages, and the birds were trilling. I hate seeing birds in cages. I had an urge to open the cages and let them out.

We cruised through the jungle of plants without being attacked by tigers, and into an even wider foyer. There was a desk there. There was a young black woman behind it. She appeared fresh and professional and very nice-looking. Her dark brown eyes were as smooth and cool as refrigerated chocolates. She smiled at us as we walked up. She gave Cason an extra smile, and I thought she showed him more teeth than she showed us.

They were nice teeth, by the way.

Cason told her why we were there. There were a series of chairs along one side of the foyer, and we went over there to sit while she pushed a button on her phone. She talked quietly for a moment over the intercom.

"You can go in right away," she said.

As we passed her desk, Cason gave her a wink, and she smiled.

Just before we went inside, I said to Cason, "Are there any women who don't like you?"

"Yes," Cason said. "But it's a short list."

40

Kincaid's office was about the size of an airport and there was some nice furniture there, including a large couch, and there were paintings on the walls. The paintings were mostly of birds, though there were some that looked to be nothing more than splashes of color. Maybe the splashes were birds too.

Kincaid was sitting behind a large desk, and he looked older than sixty by no more than a hundred years. He was white-headed and his face seemed to have collapsed at some point and been blown back into shape with a water hose. He hardly had a chin and there was a clear tube running up from behind the desk that ended in a little fitting that went into his nose. He was on oxygen. The gray suit he was wearing was like a tent that folded up around him. I saw that he was in a motorized chair.

At a smaller desk nearby was a middle-aged woman in a blue dress. She was stout of build but nice-looking. Her hair was tinted blonde and well sprayed. She looked healthy enough to wrestle a steer.

She got up from behind her desk with a catlike grace and came out to greet us, shook our hands, told us her name was Miss Sara Clinton. She directed us to chairs in front of Kincaid's desk the way a waitress shows you your table.

"Which one of you is Mr. Statler?" Kincaid asked. When he spoke, the words fell out of his mouth as slow and gentle as a sweet afternoon rain. Hearing him talk made me sleepy.

Cason said, "That's me."

"I spoke with you over the phone."

"Yes."

"These are your associates, of course."

"Yes," Cason said, gesturing to each of us. "Leonard Pine and Hap Collins."

"Hap," he said, "that's an unusual name. Is it short for anything?"

"Hap," I said.

He smiled a little. The act of talking seemed to tire him out. "You mentioned my son. I wanted to know what you had to say, but what can be said? He's gone, and the people who did it are, according to the police, all dead."

Cason nodded. "That's true, sir. We have been asked by the mother of a boy who was killed with one of the women, Mini—"

"I know who she is," he said, not wanting to hear the rest of the name. "I followed the case, obviously." His voice was less gentle now, like the rain had suddenly been disturbed by thunder. "You aren't lawyers are you?"

"No," Cason said.

"Good."

"Why would we be lawyers?" Leonard asked.

"I don't know for sure," he said, "but I had this sudden feeling you might be, that maybe you were trying to tie me to the whole mess, a civil suit. Well, I thought maybe all of you were lawyers but you."

He nodded at me.

I wasn't sure if that was a compliment or an insult.

Leonard leaned over to me, said, "I look like a lawyer."

I thought: Let's get your deerstalker and have you put it on, and then we'll see how much you look like a lawyer.

"Why would you think that, sir?" Cason said. He was using all of his buttery personality, and it was working. I suppose it was the reporter in him, experience with others. He hadn't been buttery when we first met him.

"Because that Mini you mentioned. Her stepfather tried to tie me to her death. I would gladly have killed her, and all of the others, myself, but I doubt carrying an oxygen tank and having to ride around in this chair would have made me much of an assassin."

"How did he try to tie you to them?"

"I'm not really sure what he was thinking, but he decided somehow we were responsible, like we had paid to have it done. Ridiculous."

"Well, we have nothing to do with him," I said.

"We represent a Mrs. Christopher," Cason said. "We're trying to find information concerning the death of her son, trying to figure what connection there could be to him having been killed."

"You're detectives?"

"Mostly," Cason said.

"Wrong place, wrong time," Kincaid said.

"What?" Cason said.

"The boy," Kincaid said. "He must have been in the wrong place at the wrong time. Should have kept better company."

"Perhaps," Cason said.

"Those are the hard facts. My only son was killed by these animals. Anyone who would associate with them is no better than the animals they were. Vampires! Seriously, now."

"Animals actually have a much more polite and less devious agenda," I said.

"I agree," Kincaid said.

"It's just that we've been hired to investigate," I said, "so we're asking some questions. It's not meant to be personal. We're just trying to fit some shoes, so to speak."

"I'm not Cinderella. Whatever you're asking, whatever shoes you're laying out, my feet don't fit."

"Well," I said, "long as we're on a fairy-tale theme, you might call us Goldilocks. We have to try out different things to find out which ones are just right. It's our job, nothing more."

He grinned at me. His teeth, though clean and shiny, looked loose in his mouth. "You're thinking that I didn't kill them, but that I have money, and I had them killed. The ones who got off, I mean. You're thinking like the stepfather. I didn't do anything to them. I should have. I wanted to. But I didn't know how to go about it. Besides, the law took care of the actual killer, and fate took care of the accomplices and the young man who was in the wrong place at the wrong time."

"The stepfather, Bert," I said. "He's dead too."

"How unfortunate. He came to me trying to tie me to the death of this . . . Mini. He was certain I had something to do with it. He wanted money. I told him where he could go, and he must have gone there. I haven't heard from him, or of him, again, until just now."

"The others, way the law took care of them," Leonard said. "That satisfy you?"

"No. But the fat queer got what she deserved in prison. The others got theirs as well. As I said. Fate. I'm not satisfied with the law, but fate has satisfied me as much as a man can be satisfied in a situation like this."

"Do you have any idea how the others might have died?" I said, trying to make the question sound as casual as if asking him if he wanted a back massage.

"No. Why would I? I was told they were all dead. My assumption is they died due to their connections, others who were as crazy as they were. If I knew who those people were, provided I didn't think they too were somehow connected to my son's death, I might throw them a parade. Well, gentlemen. I'm a busy man. I have a nap to take. It's when I do my best thinking."

Miss Clinton, who had gone behind her desk to sit, got up and came over and directed us toward the door. She even took my arm and led me. Why the hell was I getting the bum's rush? Why not Leonard or Cason? Was it because I didn't look like a lawyer?

We were hurried out into the foyer, where the receptionist waited behind her desk. As we passed she looked at Cason the way a dog looks at a pork chop. He looked back at her and smiled and then she smiled again. There was enough sexual tension in the air between them you could have sparked a candlewick to flame.

We stopped in the jungle section with Miss Clinton. There were still no tigers. The birds were screeching loudly, making me a nervous wreck.

Miss Clinton said, "He doesn't mean to be rude, but questions about his son, they disturb him."

"He seemed awfully hostile for someone happy with how things turned out, the killers getting theirs," I said.

"That was his only son. His only child. He's dead and he isn't coming back, and it was all because of some kind of prank, or belief, whatever you like to call it, son."

"Hap. Or Mr. Collins," I said. "I don't go by son."

"Don't be cute with me. You're not that cute."

I thought: And you're not old enough to be my mother, so don't call me son. But I didn't say it aloud. I was kind of glad she thought I looked that young. You got to take compliments where you find them, even if the remark wasn't actually meant as one.

"Thing is," she said, "any discussion of his son always upsets him."

"Then why did he let us come discuss it with him?" Cason

asked. "We're not here to harass him. Just to find out information that might help our client."

"He wanted to hear anything that might be about his son, and he wanted to hear nothing. Do you understand?"

"We regret if we upset him, or you," I said. "You seem very loyal."

"Loyal? That's not the word. He's my ex-husband."

"Your ex-husband," Leonard said. "So, the boy was your son?"

"No. Mr. Kincaid divorced me, married . . . another woman. She died of throat cancer . . . smoked like a chimney. I was his personal assistant when we were married, and I stayed that way."

"I can respect that," I said.

"Can you? You can? Well, I don't need your respect."

"Well, you don't get mine," Leonard said. "I think you're a goddamn doormat."

"You don't have to be rude," she said.

"Duh," Leonard said. "Of course I don't have to be. Neither do you. We are grown-ass adults and we both decided to be rude."

She left then, went past the squawking birds and back through the doors that led into Mr. Kincaid's office. She was a real fast walker.

Leonard looked at me. "You respect that shit? I think she's goddamn pathetic."

"I think it's kind of sweet," I said.

"You two hash that out," Cason said. "These damn birds are making me crazy."

We stood there while Cason went back to the desk and talked to the receptionist. When he came back he had her name written on the back of Kincaid's business card.

41

Since Cason had a date with the Kincaid secretary, Lateesha, we thought staying at Constance's place might be bad form, so we rented a room in the Holiday Inn Express near the airport. It had two beds and a rollaway; we left that death trap for Cason.

Cason didn't come back that night, so we sat around and watched television and went to bed late, like parents worried about their boy who had passed his curfew. In the morning, we went downstairs and looked at the free breakfast and understood why it was free, so we walked to a restaurant next door.

As we walked, Leonard said, "If Cason doesn't show soon, he's going to have to find a ride home. I'm not taking that mother-fucker in to raise."

"I thought you said he was loyal, and—"

"Oh, shut up."

We were going inside the restaurant when Cason came up. Out in the lot, we saw Lateesha driving away in a red sports car.

"Good to see you," I said. "But we didn't come here to serve as a dating service."

"Oh, I got that date all on my own."

Cason held up a disc.

"What's that?" Leonard said.

"A list of all of Kincaid's clients," he said. "Lateesha got it for me off her computer. It occurred to me that—and I know this will be hard to believe—Kincaid might be lying."

"What has the world come to?" I said.

"I'm going to send it to Mercury, have him cross-check it and see if there's anyone on it that might be someone who would do Kincaid a favor. So to speak."

"The old organized crime figure on the accountant sheet trick," I said.

"That's it," Cason said.

The greeter came over and guided us to a booth in the back, which is what we asked for. Soon as we were seated a thin waitress who looked as if it would be all right with her if everyone who ever wanted to eat in a restaurant was dead, arrived and took our coffee orders and went away.

"Mercury can do that?" I said. "He has that kind of list available to him?"

"He has a list of lists," Cason said. "If there are people on this disc that cross-check as criminals, or are associated with criminals . . . We can check. It might lead to something, and it might lead to nothing. But it seems like this baby"—he held up the disc—"has made the trip worthwhile. It's more than Kincaid would ever tell us just by asking."

"Lateesha get anything out of this?" I asked.

"About six inches of dick and a marvelous breakfast," Cason said.

"Six inches and about ten feet of bullshit is what I figure," Leonard said.

"I'm not the world's best person to be around women," Cason said. "And the worse thing is, if I really get interested in them and they lose interest in me, which seems to happen as I tend to get preoccupied with things—"

"Like more women," I said.

"That would be one of the preoccupations, yes," Cason said. "But if they lose interest in me, I become a half-ass stalker if I don't watch it. It's hard for me to let go."

"So you have an inferiority complex," Leonard said.

"Could be," Cason said.

"What about Constance?" Leonard said.

"I'm seeing her next weekend," Cason said.

"What about Lateesha?" I said.

"Constance Saturday, Lateesha Sunday."

"Do you take vitamins?" I asked.

"Push-ups and clean living," Cason said.

Driving home, Cason and Leonard talked about this and that. I tuned out and thought about Kincaid. If he had done anything to get rid of those associated with Godzilla, and her crime, I had a hard time figuring out what made him bad and us good. I had his money and resources I might have done the same thing. Hell, without his money I had done that kind of thing in the past, and Leonard was with me and he was proud of it.

So why did his shit stink and ours smelled like perfume?

And Bert had an idea, maybe a guess similar to ours, that Kincaid might have done the daughter in, and since he had lost all that money to the kitties, maybe he thought he could get some out of Kincaid. Only thing was, Kincaid hadn't bit, and he may not have bit because he may not have been guilty. Or the only card Bert was holding was a guess, and Kincaid knew it. He struck me as a shrewd and intuitive man. And Miss Clinton, she didn't seem like a slacker either. But the bottom line was, Bert was dead. Why would Kincaid bother to have him killed? Or had he. And if not, who did?

No answers presented themselves.

42

By the time we got back to LaBorde, Leonard and Cason had become buddies. They both had been in the military, in different wars, but they had some similar experiences. When Cason got out of the car at his place, Leonard got out and they hugged.

When Leonard got back in and we were tooling along, I said, "That was some hug."

"Don't worry," Leonard said. "You're still number one."

We drove to Marvin's office. The girl at the bicycle shop was standing in the open doorway. She was dressed warm today. The weather had turned cold and there was a hint of rain on the air. She had on a woolen cap and her hair cascaded out from under that. She wore a leather bomber jacket with a sheep's wool collar, blue jeans, and some big boots with fur trim. The only thing missing was the sled dogs.

In the office, Marvin had a small heater plugged into the wall and he was sitting by it in his rolling chair.

"Can't find the money for some real heat?" I said.

"Central air is out," Marvin said. "And I can't afford to fix it. We get through with this case, I can. I may even get a new coffeepot and a better water cooler."

We pulled the client chairs over by the heater. Leonard said, "Are you hinting that we should hurry up?"

"No," he said, "but a conclusion at some point in time would be nice."

"We're starting to believe Kincaid was looking for vengeance for his son," Leonard said, "and he knew someone whose accounting business he took care of was also someone who, for a fee, could take care of business for him."

"You think that because Brett thinks that?"

"No," Leonard said. "Because it's logical."

"Another thing," I said, "Bert tried to blackmail Kincaid. Kincaid admitted that. I think Bert was guessing Kincaid had Mini and Mrs. Christopher's boy killed. He may not have seemed smart, but when it got right down to it, he could have had things figured out. Kincaid may have had him whacked. He knows the right people, and he makes millions for them on their taxes and accounts. He might be able to have them to do him a favor. Or pay them for one.

"Actually, it's all guesswork for right now, but it's all we got. Frankly, I haven't ruled out June either. She had money too, and she didn't like Mini, and how much she liked her brother is up for debate. She struck me as a hard ass in a soft-ass body."

"But you have no proof that anyone did anything?" Marvin said.

"We do have something that might give us some proof by way of our new BFF, Cason."

We filled Marvin in on all that had gone on. Told him about how Cason got the disc with the names on it.

When we finished, he said, "Cason got two pieces of ass in as many days?"

"Gets two this coming weekend as well," I said.

"I knew I hated that guy," Marvin said.

"You're married, and I might as well be," I said, "so it's of no interest to us."

"Okay, we're married, but damn, I'm jealous."

"All right," I said. "Me too. And Leonard here, I think he was hoping him and Cason might play a little grab-ass."

"It was merely an affectionate hug between comrades," Leonard said.

"About the case?" Marvin said.

"Cason is having the disc checked," I said, "and we'll get back to you."

Marvin said, "You know, guys, I don't want to be paranoid here, but I'm starting to look over my shoulder."

"You think we're in danger?" I said.

"I don't know," Marvin said. "But if Kincaid is responsible for Bert's death, it doesn't take much to piss him off. Why would he bother? It's just one more death that might tie itself to him. He could have let it go and probably been better off."

"That may not be his way," I said. "He strikes me as a man that likes to win at whatever game he's playing, and from the looks of his office digs, he has the money to make the kind of arrangements he wants for most anything next to a body transplant."

Marvin got up and poured himself a cup of coffee, came and sat back down.

"So, how do we play it?" he said.

"I'm not one for quitting," Leonard said.

"Here's my thought," I said. "Best thing for us to do is to keep poking our noses in other people's business and find out if someone will come out and play."

43

I was lying in bed with Brett, and I had told her about our day and the day before. Leonard was downstairs sleeping on the couch. From where I lay I could see the window and the night sky. It was a velvet-soft night. No rain.

"How are things between Leonard and John?" she asked.

"John's being taught that his sense of future direction ought to include deep desire for a woman's vagina."

"Who's teaching him?"

"His brother."

Brett shook her head. "Families can be a mess."

I reached over and took her hand. "I'm gonna change the subject a little."

"That sounded ominous."

"I know you have a child, a grown child," I said, "but have you ever thought about starting a family with someone else?"

"Someone else?"

"Yes."

"Who would that someone else be?"

"Oh, I don't know. Someone off the street. Someone about my height and weight and general disposition."

"You're serious?"

"I guess I am."

Brett lay without speaking for a long time. "I have thought about it, Hap. I've told you how much I love you, and how I stand by you. But . . . if we had a kid, there's no way you could do what you do."

"I could quit. Though I'm not sure what I'm quitting, since I don't know what my job is."

"You know exactly what I mean, Hap. Don't act coy."

"I think I could actually finish college."

"You tried last year and quit."

"I wasn't motivated enough."

"Now you are?"

"I could try. Unlike just about everyone else, I really had a good family. I know how to be a father. I would be good at it."

"Your lifestyle isn't exactly conducive to tricycles and soccer games and PTA meetings. You'd do all right for a while, and then you'd be . . . you know, back out there with Leonard. I don't know if I could manage it. I have a grown child that drives me crazy. I don't even know if I could have another one. I'm probably too old."

"We could find out," I said.

She reached out and patted my cheek gently. "I don't think so, baby. I love you. I do. But, Hap . . . I don't think so."

44

Morning came, and downstairs I found Brett making coffee. I said, "Where's Leonard?"

"I sent him to his place."

"Sent him?"

"To get his stuff. His rent plays out in the next couple of days. He doesn't need to be staying in some rat hole, and besides, I like having him around."

"I like having him around too . . . but not that much."

"It's temporary. Me and him talked."

"He has enough money right now to rent or put down dough on a good place, he just hasn't done it. He's cheap."

"He's not ready for that. Not with the way things are with John."

"And things may never get better," I said.

"But they might. And if they don't, he'll move on. Leonard's a survivor."

"He is at that."

"What we talked about last night," she said. "I been thinking."

"That's all right," I said. "I was having a sentimental moment."

She put her arms around me. My hands cupped her buttocks.

"How long before he gets back?" I asked.

"Let me start the coffee, then let's go upstairs and see if you can make a hole in one before he shows."

I let go of her. She turned off the coffee. She took my hand. We went upstairs.

Fore!

45

The case didn't exactly die on us after that, but it went a little south for a while while we waited on Mercury to cross check things. Me and Leonard spent time at the little gym where we had a membership, and it was a cold place to be, as the heating wasn't enough to warm up a mouse.

We were often the only people there. The owner was a big fat man whose only exercise was sitting in a chair near the door and taking money or, as in our case, checking memberships. The gym wasn't pretty, but it served our needs. It had a heavy bag, which I hate, and a speed bag, which I love, and it had a good mat we could spar on and throw each other down on. I noticed that when I was thrown it hurt more than it had just a couple years back. Time seemed to have made the ground harder, even if it had a mat over it.

The cold made us train briskly, skipping rope, pounding the heavy bag, punching the speed. After that we sparred a little.

It was good and fun to work out with the weather going wonky, dropping uncharacteristically down to seventeen at night, and in the high twenties during the day. Weather like that, you had to keep moving. Even as we sparred our breath puffed little white clouds. It was odd weather for East Texas, the sort that came once in a blue moon.

We finished up by going over self-defense drills, doing them pretty rough, to make sure we weren't slacking, then we did our groundwork, so we would be ready if we had to end up there, then we went into the cold shower room with our feet freezing on the tile, took hot showers not only to clean up, but to warm up, got dressed, and drove home.

When we got there, Cason's car was parked out front with the engine running, the exhaust pumping into the cold air. After we parked, he climbed out, dressed in a bomber jacket and slacks and a shirt and tie. He held up a folder.

"Mercury," he said.

I invited him inside, sat him at the kitchen table with Leonard, and made some hot tea.

"How British," Cason said, as he took his cup of tea.

"I see that dress code has kicked in," I said.

"Yeah," Cason said, "it has."

"About the file," Leonard said.

The file lay in the center of the table. Cason tapped it with a finger.

"Mercury cross-checked names, and there are people on the list that are kind of scary, including a nasty guy named Cletus Jimson."

"Oh yeah," Leonard said. "He's a sweetheart."

"You know him?" Cason said.

"We've crossed paths," I said. "He doesn't like us."

"We're often misunderstood," Leonard said.

"Do you think Kincaid could have hired him to do it?" Cason asked. "Kill those folks?"

"Cletus doesn't do that sort of work, he has it done," I said. "I suppose Kincaid could have contacted him about a little help, though."

"Jesus Christ," Leonard said. "I hope it isn't Vanilla Ride."

"Who?" Cason said.

"You don't want to know," I said. "Those other devil head murders. Ones up in Oregon and so on. When were they?"

Cason told us.

I said, "Those are too long ago for Vanilla. She'd have been in the womb. She's not that old. And even if I add five or six years to what I think her age is, she's still too young. I hope."

"That's a relief," Leonard said. "I keep thinking we'll see her again, and may not like it when we do."

"I don't think she and Jimson are on that good of terms," I

said. "Not the way I remember it. So, taking that fact and adding her youth to it, I think we can safely say, no Vanilla Ride."

"Money and need make strange bedfellows," Leonard said. "And I don't think Cletus has forgotten us. He had these others killed for Kincaid . . . hell, maybe even June, and it all leads to us sticking our noses into his business, he might decide to put us on the list, and considering our past history, perhaps he'd do it with a certain amount of enthusiasm. But that's private. You don't need to know any more than that. He doesn't like us."

I nodded.

Cason had been watching us in a tennis-match fashion. Head first to one, then the other. "So, I'm sort of out of this part of the conversation," he said.

"Yep," I said. "We don't want to explain that part of our past. But it's possible Jimson did Kincaid a favor, if he got something big in return."

"Should we talk to him?" Cason said.

"That could be tricky," I said. "It's like stirring up a snake. He's sleeping all quiet like, hibernating maybe, and we go in there with a stick and twist him around with it, piss him off, and we are in for some shit when he may not have anything to do with this. So, we could get bit for nothing."

"I got the impression you boys get bit a lot," Cason said.

"That's why we don't want to get bit again," I said.

Leonard looked at me, then looked away. He said to Cason: "I don't mind talkin' to him. We need to, we will. But is he the only one on your list? I think before we stir him up, we got to decide if these murders connect somehow with the murders in Oregon and the like. I think Jimson would kill his mother if he thought he could get a nickel for her bloody Tampax, but I don't think he'd go out of the South. He's sort of regional."

"Yeah," I said, "his territory is East Texas and western Louisiana mostly. I reckon he could do some business outside of this area, but I don't know the business he'd do would be that sort of thing. He's got his niche here. He's got contacts and has the right people paid off, but up north, not so much would be my guess. What I think Jimson likes is being a big frog in a small pond. It's his comfort zone."

"Anyone else on that list suspect?" Leonard asked.

Cason nodded. "Couple others, but the thing is they aren't that big-time. They're little operations, and I got a feeling our killer, our Devil Red, is well trained and works for big money. That's why I thought of Jimson. He's much bigger time than the other two jokers."

"Where are they from?" I asked.

"Midwest," Cason said.

"Kincaid isn't afraid to do business with bad people," Leonard said. "Keep their taxes clean and fresh. So that makes it even more likely he would have been willing to make some kind of deal to get even for his son."

"Maybe he just does their taxes and tells them how to save on weather stripping their homes," I said.

"Yeah, right," Leonard said.

"If Kincaid did arrange it, I'm not sure I blame him for wanting to get even," I said. "Losing first a daughter to drugs, then a son to murder is bound to weigh on and mess up the mind—"

"Wait a minute," Leonard said. "I just had a flash. Detectives like to call it inspiration."

"Yeah," I said. "What do you call it?"

"The drug-dead daughter," Leonard said. "What do we know about her?"

"I think the whole she's dead part about covers it," Cason said.

"Let's look into it," Leonard said.

"May I ask why?" I said.

"Yes," Leonard said. "You can ask, but I got nothing to say about it yet. I may be full of shit."

"All right," Cason said. "We can check on her. I'll get Mercury on it."

46

After Cason left, we called Marvin and asked if he could set up a meeting with Jimson. The whole thing about telling Cason we didn't want to see Jimson really meant we didn't want Cason in on it. We had a history with Jimson. All bad. We didn't want to put Cason on Jimson's doo-doo list.

We sat around for about an hour, then Marvin called us back.

"What'd he say?" I said, pressing my cell phone to my ear while standing at the kitchen window, looking out at the yard, the house beyond. It had turned off clear and the sun was out, but there was ice in little spots where the water ran out of the grass and collected along the concrete walk at that side of the house. If I was married to Brett and had a child, the most I'd have to think about today was maybe going to work and coming in to read the papers and play with the kid. It was a pipe dream, but I liked it.

"He said he didn't want to see you," Marvin said.

"That's not nice."

"No, it isn't."

"I don't know about you," I said, "but my iddy-biddy feelers are crushed to the bone."

"Mine too, but that's what he said. He also said eat shit and die."

"You're exaggerating."

"Yeah. Actually, I didn't talk to him. But the message from his associate, one of his bodyguards, was pretty much in that ballpark."

I turned to Leonard. "Jimson doesn't want to see us."

"Then we should respect his wishes," Leonard said.

47

Within fifteen minutes we were on our way to the little burg of No Enterprise. It wasn't much of a place, a four-way stop with a string of buildings here and there, but for some odd reason, Jimson lived over in that area and did a lot of his business in a little service station that also had sodas and liquor and snack goods, had some tables in the back with some chairs, and sold hamburgers. Good burgers, bad fries. The pie was good too.

Jimson spent a lot of time there in the afternoons with his goons. If he wasn't there, well, we'd have chocolate pie with meringue. If he was there, we'd probably have it anyway. Maybe a hamburger. Me and Leonard, we believed in living large. It's just how we roll.

It took us a little over half an hour to get there because there were some low spots in the highway and water ran across those, and in this weather they had frozen, making an occasional shiny ribbon of ice across the road. Mostly it took us a while because Leonard had a new country music CD and he wanted to hear all of it before we stopped. He said, "They get rowdy, and I get killed, I like to know I heard all of it."

"You're dead, what does it matter?"

"It's the idea of it," he said. "I just want to know I consumed it all, at least once."

"You've heard it before."

"But it's a different collection of the same songs. I like that they're in a different order."

"Jerry Lee Lewis singing country sounds pretty much like Jerry Lee Lewis singing country in any order."

"Oh yes, and oh so good."

I had to agree. He told me to shut up and played the CD.

We were both armed. I had my permit pistol, and Leonard had a sawed-off shotgun without a permit fitted inside his long coat. He flared the coat back, he could pull it out of there faster than you could blink.

When we arrived the café part was absent of Jimson and thugs. In fact, it was absent of any patrons. There was a guy at the counter, and when we sat down back there, he said, "You got to come up here to get menus."

I got up and got us a couple of menus. I noticed there was a large jar of pickled eggs on the counter and a small jar with a kid's photo on it and a request for money due to burns received in a car wreck. I put a buck in the can and took the menus back to where Leonard had picked seats. There was a door back there that was an emergency door. It didn't open from the outside. Anyone came in, they had to come in the front door and come along the path between the counter and the tables to reach us. There was a wide row of glass to our left, but we were sitting at a table where I had my back against the wall, and had a bit of wall to protect me. Leonard was point man. Anyone came up, he could see them through the glass, and if need be he could cut down on them with that shotgun, start pumping out loads.

We ordered two hamburgers from the guy when he came over. He was a little nasty-looking for a man who worked as a cook. His fingers were nicotine stained and his teeth were the same. In fact, where the stains were missing, black decay had filled in between his teeth like dirt washed down from a hill.

Leonard said, "Two hamburgers, no fries, hold the hepatitis."

"What?" the man said.

"I mean wash your hands. I like to think that's nicotine, but for all I know it could be from you sticking your finger up your ass."

"You guys leave," he said.

"We work for the health department, mister," I said. "I wouldn't push it."

He looked at me, said, "Show me your credentials."

"We don't carry any. We're here to surprise people, not let them know we're coming."

"Credentials just show who you are," he said. "I'm already surprised."

"True," Leonard said, "but you've got on my bad side. Go wash your hands."

The man studied Leonard for a moment, figured quite correctly we weren't with the health department, but he wasn't really sure about throwing us out. Especially Leonard, who had a kind of lazy look that said "I'd love to kill you very much."

"All right," he said. "Two hamburgers."

"After you wash your hands," Leonard said. "And I even think or consider you might spit in my food or mess with it, I will personally see you get some big demerits. And on top of that, I will hold your face against the stove until it cooks your nose off."

"No need to get nasty," the man said.

"Your fingers are nasty enough," Leonard said.

The man went away.

I said, "Leonard, why do you always try to make friends wherever we go?"

"Our man Jimson comes here all the time, so he's got to tip Shit Fingers something or another now and then to use the space, and I figure whatever he tips him is big enough to buy some loyalty. I figure Shit Fingers is in the back there now, punching him up on the cell phone. I figure it's a way to pull Jimson out of the Jacuzzi and get him on the road."

"You know, you're not as dumb as you look."

48

Our hamburgers arrived, and about the same time we saw Jimson and two of his goon balls push through the door, start toward us. Leonard turned so that he was facing that direction. He had his hand inside his coat. Things went south, he'd have the shotgun up and ready. I put my hand in my coat and felt for the automatic, but to tell you the truth, I wasn't sure I could use it, way I'd been lately. I hoped I could at least talk tough.

Jimson was a fortyish guy who looked as if he was trying to smooth his image with expensive clothes. He was wearing a tan fedora, a very nice brown leather coat over a maroon sweater, and tan slacks so tight you wanted to yell "snake."

With him were two men that couldn't look sophisticated if they were wearing tuxes and monocles. One of them was so muscular he looked as if he had been pumped up with air. The other was leaner, and he carried his right hand close to him with his palm folded back, his coat slightly pushed. He'd be the shooter, the big man with the muscles would be the hitter.

As Jimson walked toward us, he turned to Shit Fingers, said, "You're right, they're not the health department. More like sewer."

Jimson sat at the table near us and looked at us like we were wild animal exhibits. Leonard had turned completely around in his chair. He wouldn't even need to take the shotgun out of his coat. All he had to do was lift and shoot through fabric. A shot from that sawed-off and Jimson would be mixed in with the pickled eggs.

"Fancy meeting you here," Leonard said.

"Yeah," Jimson said, "imagine that. Last time I seen you guys I didn't like it, and now I see you again, I don't like it some more."

"Is that line out of the movies?" Leonard said.

"That's an original," Jimson said. "I got a feeling you boys didn't just come over for a hamburger."

"Well," I said, "there's the pie."

Jimson smiled. "Yeah. There is the pie. So, I get a call from Marvin Hanson, a guy I don't like much, but knows me all right, and he says can his boys come see me. And you know what I say?"

"No," Leonard said.

"That's right. I say no. And then you know what?"

"Pray tell," Leonard said.

"You show up anyway."

"Not at your house," Leonard said.

"At my spot."

"Here?" Leonard said. "Really? This is your spot?"

"You been hasslin' my man over there." He nodded at Shit Fingers. "He kind of keeps me an open office here. I let you hassle my man, what kind of reputation I got with the locals?"

"What do you get out of him letting you have your office here?" I said.

"Pie."

"All right," I said. "I can see that."

Leonard nodded.

"Look, I don't know what you two assholes want, but I got nothin' to do with nothin' you're dealin' with."

"Now, how would you know that, when we haven't told you what we're dealing with? We could be selling Girl Scout cookies for all you know."

"Them's some good cookies," said the man with muscles.

Jimson turned and glanced at him. Muscles looked embarrassed, then tried to look as serious as a heart attack.

"I come here 'cause my man there called," Jimson said, "and I come here to show you guys I'm not afraid of you, that you ain't got no mojo on me. You dig on that?"

"I think 'dig' went out with the beatniks," Leonard said.

Jimson sighed. "You don't even try to work with a man when

he's trying to work with you. I wanted, I could rub you guys out. I still owe you a shitstorm that didn't never come down."

"Actually," I said, "you threw a lot of shit our way, but we sort of threw it back."

"I'm talkin' about what I could have done."

"Woulda, coulda, shoulda," Leonard said. "That was then, and this is now."

"You fellas don't want this," Jimson said. "You don't want me mad."

"Do we look nervous?" Leonard said.

Leonard didn't. Me, I wasn't so sure about.

"We made you mad before, and we're still standing," Leonard said.

"I thought you made a deal to stay out of my business if I stayed out of yours," Jimson said.

I nodded. "It's a deal we like, stayin' out of each other's business, but we're thinkin', considerin' what we know lately, maybe your business is in our business again. And if it is, well, we got to come say howdy."

"And what in the hell business could that be?" Jimson said.

Leonard said, "You know, I'm gonna pause and eat this hamburger. It's better when it's warm. Hey, Shit Fingers. Come over here."

Shit Fingers was behind the counter. He looked at Jimson. Jimson nodded.

Shit Fingers came out from behind the counter, over to Leonard.

"Let me see those hands," Leonard said.

Shit Fingers showed them to him. They had been washed.

"All right, go on about your business," Leonard said.

I looked at Jimson. He was starting to fume. That's the way Leonard wanted him. He liked people he was dealing with mad, especially when he was trying to find something out. Me too. They were more likely to mess up, reveal something they shouldn't. They were easier to read when they were angry. It's the way we worked. Either that or kicking their ass. Subtlety was not our long suit.

Muscles said, "You want me to fuck 'em up, boss?"

Jimson shook his head. "I don't know you can."

Muscles looked hurt, the way a kid might if you told him his drawing of the sky and a moon looked like a boat on the ocean.

"Here's the thing," Leonard said. "We got this client, and our client has a problem. Someone she knows, family, was murdered, and there were other murders, and they're all connected by a little symbol. A devil's head. Red. Left at the scene of the murders. You know anything about that?"

"No."

Leonard said, "Oh, Shit Fingers. I'll have a slice of pie. Hap?"

"Oh yeah," I said. "Big slice."

"I don't see how this has anything to do with me," Jimson said.

"Got that whole Kincaid-does-your-taxes thing going," Leonard said.

"Yeah, and I got a grocer, this filling station where I buy my gas and do my business, and I got a mechanic and a plumber, and a girl on Fridays comes over and pulls my dick so I don't have to."

"So you got nothin' for us?" I said.

"If I had, why would I give it to you? You come in here, you insult Shit Fingers . . . I mean Toad—"

"Toad?" I said.

"We called him that in high school. I've known him a long time. Same for these two. We grew up together."

"I used to beat him up on the playground," Muscles said.

Jimson turned and looked at him. "You could have saved that."

"Sorry, Cletus. I just thought it was funny . . . as a memory. Not that I would do it now—"

"That's all right," Jimson said. "Just be quiet."

Muscles went quiet.

"Here's what I got to say," Jimson said. "I've got nothing to do with the devil head murders. Nothing. What I can say is this: I've heard of a hit person who uses that mark. The only person more deadly than this person, so they say, is this Vanilla Ride, and you've had experience with her. They're both a lot more deadly than you are. Say I wanted somethin' done, I used to go to Vanilla. She got the job done, but now me and her got this disagreement on account of you two."

"I call bullshit on that," I said. "You decided to kill her. That's the disagreement."

"Whatever. I wanted someone killed in a bad way, I might go to this devil head killer. I might go through Kincaid. I might know he can arrange it. But me, I don't want anyone killed, so I'm not doin' that. I didn't do it in the past. I got to tell you now, you boys are startin' to annoy me. You're not keepin' your side of the bargain about stayin' out of my business."

"As long as it's out of our business," I said. "That was the bargain."

"And I'm tellin' you, if my accountant is hirin' someone to knock fuckers off, it ain't through me. That's what I'm tellin' you, and that's my word."

Shit Fingers, aka Toad, brought the pie.

"Get me one too," Jimson said.

"Yeah," Muscles said. "Pie all around. And some milk. What we got here, five milks?"

Toad looked at Jimson. Jimson sighed. "Why not? More pie. Bring milk. We might as well see if anyone wants coffee."

"I'll top it off with coffee," Muscles said.

Jimson shook his head a little.

Leonard took a big bite of pie, worked it around in his mouth, and swallowed. "Any chance you might hook us up with this Devil Red killer, like maybe we act like we got a job we want that bad boy to do?"

"No."

"Come on, man," Leonard said. "Here we are sharin' pie, and you won't hook a brother up."

"I belonged to the Aryan Nations in prison, so I don't hook brothers up."

"Unless it's to fasten 'em to a chain to get dragged by a car," Muscles said.

This time the tall thin man who hadn't said a word yet grinned. It was like seeing the Grim Reaper get a chuckle.

"Oh, that's funny," Leonard said.

"Look here. I ain't into all that nigger hatin' anymore," Jimson said.

"That's big of you," Leonard said.

"Only way you might see this Devil Red dude, as you call him, is if he comes to shoot your black ass, and your white pal too."

"That's so sweet," I said. "Both of us, and in the ass."

"Look here," Jimson said. "We've had a talk. I've bought some pie."

"We're not asking you to buy our pie," Leonard said. "The milk maybe, as your man ordered that."

Jimson snapped both hands in the air, making a crosscutting motion.

"Forget it. I've got the whole goddamn bill. I just want you two to go away and stay away, and let's go back to where we were before. I'm out of your business, and you're out of mine. You jack-asses are like having seed ticks imbedded in the balls."

"All right," Leonard said. "But before we go, and before I say thanks for lunch, let me confirm some things. There is a killer who works for money who uses a red devil head as a symbol to sign his work?"

"That's what I'm told," Jimson said.

"And you're sayin', and I know you might lie to a brother, you're sayin' you've got nothin' to do with these hits?"

"If I did," Jimson said, "them crossin' your path would just be a coincidence."

"So you're sayin' you did have somethin' to do with it?" Leonard said.

"No," Jimson said. "For Christsakes, no. That was one of those hypotheticals."

"You learn that word in prison?" I asked.

"I just added an *s* to it, that's all. I have nothing to do with Devil Red. I have never had anything to do with Devil Red. I might consider havin' something to do with Devil Red in the future. Maybe the very goddamn near future."

"That a threat?" I asked.

"Hell yeah," Jimson said.

"Don't forget," Leonard said. "Vanilla Ride is a personal friend of ours."

"No need to bring that bitch into this."

"You are such a misogynist," I said. "If you can't be sweet, don't have anything to say at all."

"Yeah," Leonard said, tossin' his napkin on the table. "You're gonna talk like that, then we'll just have to leave."

He got up. I got up. I went to the fire door and pushed it. The alarm went off. I backed slowly out of it, and Leonard backed out after me. We went around by the side glass on our way to the car. Jimson, Muscles, and the Grim Reaper were watching us from the table. Well, Muscles was actually eating pie and drinking milk. Jimson and the Reaper were watching.

Toad wasn't in sight.

Nobody pulled a gun.

49

On the way home, Leonard said, "Did Jimson seem a bit grumpy to you?"

"He did."

"The guy with the big arms, he didn't worry me none. Neither did Jimson, but the quiet one."

"I call him the Grim Reaper," I said.

"Yeah, him. He's someone could be trouble."

"We'll file him away for any future associations."

"That part of the file, people that don't like us, might kill us, and just ought to be watched, is getting sizable."

"It is," I said.

"Hap?"

"Yeah."

"You feelin' better?"

"Sure."

Actually, I had no idea how I felt.

50

When I got home, Leonard took his car and went away somewhere to do Leonard things, which probably meant he was giving Brett and me time together.

Inside, Brett was sitting on the couch with her suitcase parked by her.

I closed the door and said, "Problem?"

"It's Tillie."

"You just got back from there. You said yourself you can't change her."

"I can't. She got beat up. Her pimp did it."

"Shit. How bad?"

"Bad. She'll be all right, but she's bad."

"Damn, Brett, I'm sorry."

"I got to go. I was just waiting on you."

"Why didn't you call?"

"Your phone was off."

"Oh."

"And I wouldn't have called anyway. I wanted to see you before I left."

"How'd the hospital take it?"

"They took it," she said, and stood up. "I get there, I'll give you a call."

When she stood up and came close, I could see there were tears on her cheeks.

"Long as you need, of course," I said.

We kissed and I picked up her suitcase and carried it out to her car. She kissed me again and got behind the wheel and started the engine and rolled down the window.

"You didn't offer to settle the pimp's hash for me," she said.

"No. I didn't."

"It's all right. It won't change him and it won't change her."

She smiled at me and drove away.

I went upstairs and took off my clothes and closed the blinds and put on my pajamas and got in bed. It was early afternoon and still bright out. But not with the blinds drawn. I lay back on my pillow and pulled her pillow to me. It smelled like she smelled and I liked it.

51

When my cell phone rang, I woke up and didn't know where I was for a moment. I rolled out of bed and pulled it out of my coat pocket and flipped it open.

It was Cason.

"You and Leonard ought to get together with me and Mercury," he said.

"Got somethin'?"

"Yeah. Leonard with you?"

"No. But I can hustle him up."

"When can we get together?" Cason said.

"I don't know. I'll call him, we'll call you, and we'll get together."

"Tell Leonard not to wear the hat."

We showed up at Cason's apartment, way he said. Mercury was
there with him. Leonard didn't wear the hat.

As we went inside I gave the place a once-over. It was sort of
thrown together with home-made bookshelves and an old couch
and a coffee table that looked as if it had been salvaged from the
dump. It had so many glass and cup stains on it, it almost looked
designed.

I could see the kitchen from the middle of the room, and the
sink was full of dishes. Through an open doorway I could see an
unmade bed and clothes on the floor. It reminded me of every
place either I or Leonard had lived until Brett and I got the house.
As much as was possible, she had civilized me.

Mercury had a laptop with him and he placed it on the coffee
table, and we all found a place to sit. Cason asked if we wanted
beer. Leonard took one; so did Mercury and Cason himself. I
passed.

Mercury turned on the laptop, said, "You don't need to see this
'less you want to. I can read off my notes and tell you what I got."

We agreed this was fine.

"Kincaid's daughter died of an overdose," Mercury said. "That
much you know. But she died in Oregon. Did you know that?"

"No," I said.

"Guys that got killed and had the devil head painted at the site
were all drug dealers. You startin' to see a pattern here?"

"Kincaid's daughter died of a drug overdose, and the drug

dealers she dealt with are the ones found dead with the devil heads," I said.

Mercury nodded. "And his son is killed by crazies, and the crazies die. I think the one in jail, Gonzello a.k.a. Godzilla, was the subject of a hit, but she was tougher than the hit. But when she gave the knife back, thinking she was immortal, well, she messed up. And the train accident. Who knows? Maybe that was some kind of rig too. The Christopher boy . . . Wrong place, wrong time. Probably caught and killed him and Mini somewhere else, tried to make it look like rape and robbery. However, they just couldn't resist leaving their mark. Right there in the open, thinking no one would see the connection. But they would know, and it would please them. That's what conspiracy theorists like myself call a pattern. A pattern of deaths, a pattern of markings—a signature, if you will."

"So it all does go back to Kincaid?" I said. "He wanted revenge, so he hired Devil Red to do the deed, but Devil Red couldn't resist leaving his mark. I guess someone killed my son and daughter, I'd feel pretty vengeful."

"Thing is," Cason said, "Devil Red seems to put a lot of people to sleep, all over the country. They can't all be people who've done something to the Kincaids. What Mrs. Christopher wants is whoever killed her son. She wants Devil Red, and I'm sure, if possible, she wants whoever arranged it, so the Kincaids aren't off the hook, no matter what."

52

When we arrived at my place, we were hungry. I decided on chili.

I got a wide and deep cast-iron frying pan out from under the

cabinet and put hamburger meat in it. As it fried, I black pep-
pered it.

Leonard cut up half an onion and a jalapeño, scraped that off
the cutting board into the meat. I stirred it while he got the chili
powder out of the cabinet and shook some of that in.

I let it cook for a while, and we got soft drinks and sat at the
table and smelled the chili cooking.

"So, what do you think?" Leonard said.

"I think Mercury is probably right," I said. "It's all connected,
and the thing now is, how do we get enough evidence to nail Devil
Red, and find a way not to nail Kincaid and Ms. Clinton."

"I'm not sure I care as much about them as you do," Leonard
said. "There's something about this whole thing still bothers me.
It's like an animal called Not Quite Right crawled up my ass and is
wiggling around."

"I thought you enjoyed that kind of thing."

"Wrong kind of animal."

"All right. How about we try to find evidence to nail Devil Red,
not make an effort to stick our vengeful couple, but if things shake
out that way, and we can't keep it from happening, we let it. Him
in that chair, and she his former wife, they might get off with
something light."

"She might not have anything to do with it," Leonard said.

"Oh, she did somethin', all right. She's still in love with him.
That much was easy to tell. And if anyone knows his business,
it's her."

"He dumped her, and she's still moonin' over him like a pre-
teen," Leonard said. "I don't get it."

"I think love is hard to explain, brother."

"Yeah. Well, I think it's made up."

"You do? What about John?"

"I think I was attracted to him, and him to me, and we had
certain things in common, both being queer was right up there,
and—"

"He made you laugh, right? That's what everyone always says."

"You and Brett make each other laugh. Me and John, not so much. But I think our basic attraction created love. I think love is real, but I think it's created, kind of like a smoothie."

"You are such a romantic."

"No. No I'm not," Leonard said.

The chili cooked for a long time, and we were starved when it was ready. We ate quickly, devouring huge bowls of it with crackers, and then we did seconds. Between it all, we made some general plans about going back to Houston to shake Kincaid's and Clinton's tree some, see we could get them to make a mistake, wiggle something out of the woodwork. It wasn't a plan up there with Patton, but it was a plan. We had plenty of clues now, plenty of circumstantial evidence. Thing to do was to see if our knowing what we knew made them nervous.

And then the worm turned.

53

Leonard had a lot of his stuff at my place, so we decided he could easily pack and go from there. Some of his clothes were dirty, though, so we put them in the washer, and while it churned, we sat and talked.

Sometime later, Leonard moved his clothes to the dryer and put on a fresh shirt and pants. He came back from changing, said, "I'm cravin' more of that chili."

"Help yourself," I said. I was sitting on the couch with my feet on the coffee table, glancing at one of Brett's magazines. It didn't really have anything to do with anything I was interested in, but it killed a bit of time.

"No more crackers," he said.

"Eat it without crackers."

"I like crackers."

"I like steak and baked potato, but what you have is chili, no crackers."

"I'm gonna go get some."

"You want crackers that bad?"

"It's the way you eat chili."

"You have a rule book?" I asked.

"I know things."

Leonard got his coat. "And you're out of vanilla cookies."

"Wow, wonder where those went."

Leonard put the coat on and took his deerstalker out of the pocket and put it on. I didn't say anything, but I'm sure I sighed. Going out the door, he said, "I'll be back in twenty or thirty."

"Don't screw around," I said. "We need to pack and get gone. We have people to irritate."

"I wouldn't miss that," he said.

Leonard was gone about five minutes when I realized Leonard had left his wallet on the table with his cell phone, and even his pistol. The sawed-off was there too. He had taken them out of his pants when he had changed clothes. He was driven to have those crackers and cookies and he didn't think he needed a gun to get them. A wallet with money, though. He needed that. And frankly, the idea of him being out there, and Devil Red maybe being out there, and Leonard without a gun, it unnerved me a little. I was starting to get as paranoid as Bert was.

I got his wallet and phone and my own gun, and drove over to Wal-Mart. I knew that's where he'd go. It's where he always went.

As I drove over, it started to sleet and I could see that ice was cresting the grass in yards I passed.

When I got to the lot, I cruised around, looking for his car, and I saw it and I saw him. Leonard was in the lot walking. He had his hands in his coat pockets and his head down against the sleet.

I saw a black SUV turn down the row of cars where Leonard was walking, and when I did, my heart sank.

I drove faster, but the SUV was on him, and the back side window came down, and I saw a pistol poke out of it. I honked my horn at the same time Leonard was turning, reaching under his coat—

—for nothing.

His guns were at home, on the table.

There was a blast of fire from the open window. *Snap. Snap. Snap.*

Leonard went down.

I pulled over quick and got out and fired at the dark-windowed SUV and the glass popped and made a spider design but didn't break. The SUV gunned in. They came by my position. I could see a shape inside, through the open window, but my main concentration was on the gun poking out at me. I fired once and leaped over the hood of my car. A bullet scraped something and I lay down tight behind my tire, peeked out and under.

The SUV was roaring away. I stood up and draped my gun over the roof of my car. Someone screamed. I saw a shopper pushing a cart go right behind the SUV. No shot there. No license plate either. Not that it would have mattered. They knew what they were doing. Those plates would be false.

I screamed because I couldn't do anything else.

I put the gun away and ran toward Leonard.

It seemed to take me forever to get there.

He didn't get up. He didn't move.

The lights from Wal-Mart seemed to strobe.

54

There are some things that happen to you that thicken the air around you until it is as heavy and as hard to penetrate as stone.

I don't know a better way to explain it. It's as if air and gravity are coconspirators, pulling you down. I tried to move fast, and I suppose I was moving fast, but I felt like Brer Rabbit caught up in the tar baby. The more I struggled, the worser I got.

My feet didn't know how to work, and my head wasn't thinking clearly; my brain was echoing with the sound of gunfire.

When I got to him, he was breathing. But he was bloody, and he was bad. His stupid hat was lying nearby. There was a stream of blood flowing away from Leonard's body and it was about to touch the hat. I took the hat and put it in my coat pocket.

I said, "Leonard," but he didn't so much as blink.

I touched the pulse in his throat. He was going fast.

I stood up to see a half-dozen people standing around me. And the crowd was growing.

A lady said, "I called nine-one-one."

"I hope you hit the sonofbitch," someone in the crowd said.

After that, it seemed as if I was down on my knees forever, holding Leonard's head across my knees. Then there were sirens, and lights, an ambulance and cops.

They took my gun and put me in a cop car and I sat there not able to speak, watching through the window as the ambulance with my best friend—my brother—drove away.

They let me make a call. I called Marvin. They asked me some questions. I did my best to answer them. There wasn't a lot to say.

The cops knew me. They knew Leonard. That wasn't necessarily a good thing. And they knew Marvin.

I went downtown, and my memory of that trip is all a haze. Finally they let me go away with Marvin. I had heard only one thing, a cop saying it to another cop, out in the hallway. It was about Leonard. He wasn't expected to live.

He should have had chili without crackers, I thought. Goddamn it, Leonard. If you don't die before I get to the hospital, I'm gonna kill you. Crackers and vanilla wafers. That got you shot? Maybe killed? You sonofabitch.

Don't die, goddamn it, don't die.

Shot outside Wal-Mart. How ignoble was that? A man who had fought in a war, and had fought dozens of tough customers over the years, gunned down in a parking lot.

"Who do you think?" Marvin said.

"Jimson. He was mad at us from the time before. And we just saw him again."

"And you were not endearing."

"No. It was the usual."

"Who else is on the list?" Marvin asked.

"Vanilla Ride, maybe. Devil Red. I don't know. We pulled someone's chain a little too hard this time, and someone didn't like it, or hired someone to not like it for them. They must have been scoping us out at the house. Saw Leonard alone, thought they'd take him. Come back for me. Normally, that wouldn't be an easy thing. But this time, it was."

"There's no rhyme or reason to that sort of thing," Marvin said.

"They caught us apart. We're not easy apart, but together, we're really difficult. Except this time."

"Even monkeys fall out of trees," Marvin said. "It's not always about how good you are."

"Take me by the house before the hospital. I want to get something."

. . .

Marvin parked down the street and let me out, and then he drove by, to see what he could see. I walked across two backyards and went to my back door. No one was waiting on me. I used the key and went inside.

Upstairs, I got Brett's little revolver and put it in my coat pocket. Simple gun. Light enough. No jams.

Downstairs, I looked out the back window. I could see our neighbor's fence, and nothing else.

I went to the living room, peeled the curtain on first one window, then another. The yard was empty, except for dead grass nipped over with ice.

I put my hand in my pocket and went outside and looked around. I didn't see a sniper's nest or black helicopters or Bigfoot.

Marvin coasted up front. I got in and we went away.

It had turned very icy by now, and we almost went off in a ditch once. But we made it.

As I walked into the hospital, shaken to my core, the last thing I told myself was it no longer mattered what had been going on inside of me as of late, because I was past that now.

It didn't matter.

It was behind me.

Whoever did this to Leonard was going to die.

55

They wouldn't let us see Leonard. He was in surgery. Me and Marvin sat in uncomfortable chairs in an overlit waiting room with a TV on without the sound and a lady wrapped up in a blanket sleeping in a chair across the way. From time to time, Marvin got up and made some calls to the cops and who knows who all.

When he came and sat back down, I said, "Thomas and his crony aren't out of jail, are they?"

"First thing I thought of," Marvin said. "Answer is no."

"No idea of anyone else?"

Marvin shook his head. "Folks saw the SUV. Heard shots. But didn't really see anyone, same as you. A woman got the license, but—"

"It's not to an SUV."

"That's right. It's not. It was stolen from a car that's already been traced. They must have taken it off the car tonight. Quick and fast. They've already traded the license plate on their car back by now, tossed the other one."

"Shit. I should have been with him. We're together, shit like that doesn't happen."

"Of course it does. You two have just been lucky. All of us, we just been lucky. We've all been shot, nearly killed. Just not as bad as Leonard got tonight."

"I'm thinkin' maybe Jimson," I said. "We rode him pretty hard."

"Possibility."

"And then there's Devil Red."

"Really?" Marvin said.

"Could be. Jimson implied he knew how to contact Devil Red. Like maybe he could hire him, he wanted to. Or maybe we got Kincaid stirred when we were in Houston and he put Devil Red on us. I don't know. Anyone say anything about finding a drawing, something with a devil head on it?"

"No. But that might be information even my buddies wouldn't tell me," Marvin said. "But, if it was Devil Red, he might not leave a warning if there's no time. Also, since the shots came from the back window, he's got help."

"That could point to Jimson," I said. "It might just be him and some of his boys."

Marvin was hesitant. "Well, when it comes to you two, there is a long list. Only thing I can say, it wasn't random, and it wasn't for robbery. They had one purpose. Shoot Leonard. And if they did that, I pretty much think you're next."

It was a long time before Leonard came out of surgery. We weren't allowed to see him then, just a glimpse as they pushed his gurney onto an elevator and took him away. He looked ashen, and when a black man looks that ashen, it's not good, not good at all.

The surgeon met with us in the break room a few minutes later. The surgeon's name was Rogers and he was out of his surgery duds and wearing some loose clothes with slip-on shoes.

We sat at a break table in plastic chairs. The room seemed too bright.

"He's pretty bad," Rogers said. "He's tough, though. I'll tell you that. I couldn't believe he'd taken those slugs, bled that much, and was still alive. He could even talk a little."

"He say who did it?" Marvin asked.

"He asked me if we found the cookies."

"The cookies?" I said. "Why that silly sonofabitch. The last thing he asked about were cookies? He never even made it inside the store."

"He was kind of out of it. He asked about a hat too. Neither meant anything to me."

I smiled. Thought: That's probably why he was shot, that hat.

"Wish I could tell you he was going to be better," Rogers said.

I held my breath.

"I can't," he said. "He could recover. Like I said, he's tough. But he lost a lot of blood, lots of trauma."

"What kind of chance does he have?" I asked.

"No way of really knowing," Rogers said. "But I'd say he's on the low end of possibilities."

"What's that mean?" Marvin said.

"This is all guesswork, gentlemen. Ten, twenty percent maybe."

"Oh, hell," I said.

"Ten, twenty percent, that's something, though," Rogers said. "It's a wait-and-see situation, not a wait-for-certain-death kind of deal. And like I said, he seems to have a lot of willpower. That's what makes someone tough. Not just muscle and flesh, but willpower."

"He'll make it," I said.

Rogers stood. "We're doing all we can."

"Do all you can and more," I said. "That's my brother in there."

56

After we talked to the surgeon, I told Marvin to go home, be with his family. I walked outside with him to his car. He opened his trunk and got out a golf club bag with clubs poking out of it. He said, "Borrow these."

I just looked at him.

"Inside," he said, "is a sawed-off pump shotgun, twelve-gauge. You might want to put it together."

"I might at that," I said.

I opened my trunk and he put the bag inside.

"We're on hospital camera, you know," Marvin said.

"I know."

I closed the trunk.

I called Brett. I waited in the parking lot till she arrived. I put the golf bag in the trunk of her car. She didn't say anything. We went up to the waiting room. We were the only ones there.

Brett was red-faced and her eyes were red too. Her hair was

tied back and her shoulders were slumped. She sat down beside me and took my hand.

"How is he?"

"No word," I said. "I think the same."

She patted my hand.

"I know you need to find out who did it," she said.

"Yeah."

"I know what you'll do when you find them."

"Yeah."

"Those weren't just golf clubs, were they?"

"No," I said.

"So, how are you gonna get who did it sitting here?"

"I want to know how he is. I want to know he's okay."

"We have phones. You sitting here doesn't change anything. You get that sonofabitch. Whatever it takes, you get him. And if you need me to help you get him, I will."

"I know," I said.

She pulled my head around and looked me directly in the eyes. "I'll stay here. You . . . you have any ideas. Any way to get ideas, anyone to get ideas from, you do it. Take my car. And when you find who did this, and I know you'll find them, show no mercy."

57

I drove over to No Enterprise. I drove carefully. There was a little park by the side of the road just outside of the city limits. I pulled over there and opened the trunk and took out the golf bag and dug in there until I found the shotgun. It was in two pieces. There was a little bag with tools in it. I put the shotgun together swiftly. There were shells in a plastic bag. I loaded the gun.

I looked up as a black Volkswagen drove by, heading back the way I had come. I hoped they weren't pulling into the park.

They drove on.

I put the bag back in the trunk and took the shotgun and laid it on the front passenger's seat and drove on into No Enterprise. There was no reason to expect Jimson to be where I hoped he was, but Shit Fingers or someone there would know. I'd get him to come there if I had to beat the information out of an innocent bystander. I might even make them drink the coffee.

When I got to No Enterprise, I saw the service station/convenience store. It occurred to me as I arrived that it might not be open. But it was. It was all night. It was the swinging spot in No Enterprise.

The lights were on, but right then it wasn't swinging.

I cruised into the lot and parked. There was a dark SUV parked in front of the store, near the door. I tried to determine if it was the one in the Wal-Mart lot, came to the conclusion it was not.

I got the shotgun off the seat and opened the door. My legs felt like lead, but I made them move anyway. I held the gun down by my side, and used my other hand to tap the revolver beneath my coat.

I walked straight to the door and went in.

No one was there.

That was alive.

I saw Jimson on the floor, his head turned funny and his mouth open. So were his eyes. His blood was all over the floor. He had one hand inside his coat. Probably reaching for a gun.

Sitting in a chair at the table was Muscles. He had his head thrown back, and his mouth was open, like something you were supposed to toss a ball into.

The thin man lay on the floor. He was on his back. He had his hand on his gun, but it wasn't drawn. He had a hole in the center of his forehead, nice and neat, like it was painted there with a paint pen. The back of his head was oozing blood. The place smelled of blood, gunfire, and feces from evacuated bowels.

I took a breath and looked around. No one. I walked over to the counter and looked behind it. Like I expected. Shit Fingers. He was dead too, crumpled on his side with his knees drawn up. His mouth was leaking blood. Blood was splattered on the cigarettes in a rack behind him.

For some reason the only thing I could think was a dedicated smoker could buy those cheap.

Blood. All of it fresh. This had just happened.

I felt the hair on the back of my neck crawl around. I took another deep breath and backed out of there.

58

I went home to get a bigger gun.

I went home to get more than one.

I went home to break into the stash upstairs. A twelve-gauge pump better than the sawed-off, and a .45 automatic pistol. I kept them inside the closet there, behind the opening in the ceiling, up in what served as an attic. Both were cold pieces. There was plenty of plastic-wrapped ammunition up there too.

Sometimes when I thought of those things up there, I felt as if a sleeping dragon were just waiting for me to call it out and use it wrong.

But this time, I was happy. Whoever had wiped out Jimson and his men, and Shit Fingers, they had been the one who shot Leonard. Had to be. Too big of a conincidence otherwise. And I had no reason to doubt that I was next on the list.

This time I couldn't wait to get my hands on those guns, to let the dragon loose.

I was thinking about all that as I drove into my drive, got out carefully, and looked around, Brett's revolver hanging loose in my hand. I thought I heard the icy grass crunch once, but I went still and waited and didn't hear it again. It could have been anything. Ice shifting. A cat or a dog running across the backyard. Anything.

Or nothing.

When I was on the porch I kept Brett's revolver in my right hand and held my keys in the left.

As I was pushing the key in, a voice said, "I wouldn't do that."

I dropped and wheeled.

Standing in the yard, wearing a long heavy duster-style coat, was a young woman with long blonde hair. In the glow of the single streetlight at the end of the drive her hair appeared to fall over her shoulders and down the front of her coat like a waterfall of butter. She had a gun in her right hand, and the hand was leveled at me, and I knew before I could even get a shot off, I'd be dead.

It was Vanilla Ride.

59

Once upon a time, Vanilla Ride had been hired to kill me and Leonard. But her employer, one Cletus Jimson, got greedy on the money he owed her for other hits, and decided to hit her together with us instead. It was a cost-cutting plan.

As it worked out, Leonard and I helped her fight them off. There was a lot of gunfire, a lot of blood, and the hit on the hitter failed.

That gave us a connection with Vanilla.

It gave me and her another kind of connection that I can't explain. Not romantic. Brett wouldn't like that, and in the long run, neither would I. But it bonded us. Still, I never really expected to see her again.

Or hoped I wouldn't.

"Hi, Hap," she said, as cheery as if we were meeting for coffee.

"So, it was you who shot Leonard."

"Don't be silly. He'd be dead. I'm not here to shoot you. I'm here with a warning."

"What do you mean a warning?"

"I'm not going to shoot you. Not unless I have to. I don't even have a silencer on my gun. I'm not here for business."

I knew she was right. She walked like a ninja and had the aim of Annie Oakley. Had she wanted, she could have killed me and I would never have known she was there. I lowered the revolver by my side, but I didn't put it away.

I said, "I'm not in the mood, Vanilla. You could kill me, maybe. But I might not die so easy."

"Yeah, you would. This is a twenty-two. Not a big caliber. But I can put a bullet where I want to standing this close. I can write my name in bullet fire on your forehead before you hit the ground."

"Yeah," I said. "But I bet you'd have to leave out one of the *l*'s."

She smiled.

"What's the warning?" I said.

"Let's start with don't open your door, because if you do, you'll get blown out into the street."

I looked at the door.

"How do you know?"

"I know. I've already checked. But I didn't disarm it. Wanted you to see me do it. I wanted you to know I'm not here to kill you."

"I was here not long ago," I said.

"And they must have been here a few minutes ago," she said. "While you were in No Enterprise looking up Jimson. Don't look so surprised. I passed you as you were going in, stopped by the road getting something out of the trunk. A gun would be my guess."

"Sawed-off. I left it on the seat. Now I wish I hadn't."

Vanilla put her gun away, came up on the porch, turned the key, and unlocked the door. I stepped back off the porch. Way back.

I saw her push the door open ever so slightly. She reached in her coat and took out a little leather parcel. She pulled a small flashlight from it and turned it on and put it in her teeth. She knelt down on one knee and removed something else from the parcel. She used it on something near the bottom of the door. A trip wire I figured. I heard a slight snip, and then another snip.

"Disarmed," she said, and pushed the door open.

Inside, just for safety measures, we turned on the lights and looked through the house. There was a bomb at the back door too.

Vanilla cut some wires like before. She said, "This would have blown you in half. Either one of them. You pushed the door open, it would have pulled the wires, and that would have pulled a trigger. You go boom, baby."

She picked the bomb up and carried it inside and placed it on the kitchen table, which is where she had put the other one. She walked into the living room, looked around. Her coat fell open and one long, black, panted leg poked out. Just for the record, she was wearing what Brett calls sensible shoes, low slung and soft and easy to move in. Even under the circumstances, I couldn't help but note she was breathtakingly beautiful—an evil wet dream with vanilla crème skin, sea blue eyes, and bloodred lipstick.

"Cozy," she said.

We stood across from each other. I still had the revolver in my hand. She said, "You really ought to put your rod away."

I put the revolver in my coat pocket.

"We never seem to meet just to say hi," she said.

"This is only the second time we've met," I said.

"But it was such an exciting meeting."

"Truth is, I don't feel like a lot of chitchat right now."

"Because of Leonard," she said.

I hesitated before I answered. "That's right. How would you know about that? How would you know to check my house for a bomb?"

"I've been watching you. I wasn't watching Leonard. I wasn't sure I was going to warn you. I was here to do it, but I wasn't sure I'd go through with it. I was down the street, parked in a car at the curb when Leonard left. I saw it was him, I stayed. I'm here to protect you, not him. Later, I followed you to the hospital. I figured things out. I know how to ask the right questions at a hospital desk without seeming nosy. I told them I was your sister. They told me whatever I asked."

"How clever of you."

"You and me, we need to sit down on the couch and talk."

"I don't feel all that chatty. Thanks for not letting me get blown up, but I got things to do."

She looked back at the kitchen. "You have anything to drink?"

"Vanilla . . ."

"No. Really. We need to talk."

60

"So," I said, when we were seated on the couch, "you were just in the neighborhood."

"You don't have any vodka?"

"No. You already asked."

"A beer?"

"Nope."

I had given her a diet soda, and she was sipping it. I was so nervous I was about to vibrate out of the room. She seemed very casual. We had turned off the main lights. She thought it a good idea, in case anyone was watching the house, waiting for it to blow.

The only light on now was the little plastic fish-shaped light plugged into the kitchen outlet over the counter. The light from it stretched into the living room, but it was faint and soft.

"You didn't get blown up, so they'll come back," Vanilla said.

"Are you Devil Red as well as Vanilla Ride?"

"Devil Red," she said. "That's a funny name."

"So is Vanilla Ride."

"That's the name I was given," she said. "Devil Red, that's made up."

"But you know who I'm talking about?"

"I do. And we can use that term if you like."

"Considering you tried to kill me before, you're awfully pleasant."

"I'm always pleasant."

"I've seen you less pleasant."

"Oh, come on, Hap. Let bygones be bygones. We made up, remember."

"We never quarreled. And still, you tried to kill me."

"Killing people for money. It's what I do."

"Look, Vanilla, my brother may be dying. Someone shot him. Someone is gonna die if I have my way. If that's you, or whoever—"

"It's not me. But it is . . ." She hesitated as she worked the words around in her mouth. "Devil Red."

"All right, now I know. I just have to find him."

She looked at me and smiled faintly. "You're not up to it, Hap. You're not up to me."

"So, why are you here? Tell me where I can find Devil Red, and let me get about my business, up to it or not."

"Don't you wonder how I knew you were in trouble?"

"It's not high on my priority list right now."

"Let's put it there. Jimson called me."

By then, of course, I knew that if she had seen me beside the road, that it was her who had given Jimson a visit. But I didn't let on. I wanted to hear it from her.

"I thought he was afraid of you," I said.

"He wanted me and him to be friends. He wanted me to know the whole thing about deciding to have me killed was just business."

"How'd you take that?" I said.

"I understood his position. I understand business. I would probably have just taken the job he was offering me if it hadn't been you."

"Why are you so concerned about my welfare?"

She studied me for a moment. "I seem to be infatuated with you."

"Me?"

"Go figure."

"I'm just a middle-aged guy going to seed. What's the attraction?"

"The same your girlfriend Brett has, I suppose. She's some looker, Hap."

"You know about her too?"

"I know all kinds of things about you. I've made it a point to know. Once I was supposed to kill you, remember? I did my research."

"Nothing like research," I said.

"Jimson, he wanted me to kill you and Leonard. I told him I didn't want to. But not before I went to see him. I was in Shreveport when I got the message through contacts. I was finishing up a little job there. Nicely done, I might add. I told him I'd come see him pretty soon."

"You got close to Jimson pretty easy. I'd have thought he was nervous about that, considering your past."

"He had never seen me before. He just contacted me. He knew how to do that through certain parties. I've known about his habits for over a year. I keep tabs on my old connections, just in case they decide to be trouble. Anyway, I went there, this little station where he spends time. He didn't know me. He saw me. He wanted to know me. That happens to me a lot."

"I bet."

"Why thank you. He had his two bodyguards with him. I sat down. He bought me a cup of coffee, started his hustle. Thought he might get some tail. And then I told him who I was."

"How'd he take it?"

"Surprised. I think he expected me to be huskier. He knew Vanilla Ride was a woman, but he had me pegged different."

"Yeah, you don't look the part. You look more like a James Bond villain."

"That's so sweet. He immediately started saying how trying to have me killed was all business, and could I take care of you and Leonard, since it didn't work out last time. He offered me double. Do you realize how many pounds of dope and how many whores he'd have to run to pay me as much as he offered me?"

"I don't know how much he offered."

Vanilla smiled. When she did, she almost looked like a cherub. "Let's just say it was a lot."

"All right, let's say that," I said. "So how's this story end?"

"Quit pulling my leg, Hap. I said I passed you. You were there. You know how it ends. I told them no, and then I shot them all."

"All of them?"

"You know that too. But, just in case you like to hear it. All of them."

"You shot the thin man first, didn't you?" I said.

"I did. He's the one that actually looked like trouble. But no. He wasn't any trouble at all. He was quick, but I was quicker. Then I shot Jimson, and then I shot the big man with all the muscles. For the hell of it, I shot the guy behind the counter. The coffee he brought me sucked."

"Yeah, coffee there isn't too good," I said. "Didn't that cause a stir, all that shooting?"

"No one else was in the place. Lucky for them. A twenty-two is pretty quiet compared to a larger gun. I didn't have a silencer. I've used them for some guns, but not this one. Doesn't work well on it. Four shots. Four dead, and I was out of there." She sat up straight when she told me that, like a proud girl in class who had just answered a hard question.

"You did that for me?"

"I did it for me. I didn't like him. And I didn't want to shoot you and Leonard. Leonard, maybe. But you, no."

"So you were supposed to come after us for Jimson. And Devil Red is after us because we've been snooping."

"That's pretty much it," she said. "But you got this figured. I can tell the way your eyes light up."

"I know some of it," I said, "but a lot of it is guesswork."

She nodded. "Jimson put Devil Red on you two as well. He wanted me for backup. The whole thing is he wanted me and Devil Red on you guys because you were so hard to kill last time."

"For that I refuse to apologize."

"This time Leonard was easy for Devil Red."

"He dropped his guard," I said. "He had shopping for cookies on his mind."

"He's tough, and so are you, but this isn't his profession, and it's not yours. Me, it's what I do."

"I bet your mother is proud."

"I wouldn't know. Way I think Jimson had it planned is he also hired Devil Red to take me out. I don't think he forgave as easy as he said, business or not. He was scared of me."

"And for good reason."

"He told me to take out Devil Red. So I think he thought he'd get rid of one connection one way or another. If it left Devil Red, not so bad. He didn't have an ugly history there. If it left me, well, he paid me off and he probably thought that would soothe things over between us and he wouldn't be worried about looking over his shoulder for me. He probably thought if Devil Red was out of the picture, that would just be one less connection to him. In time, maybe he thought he'd get me."

"So, I'm not worth as much as you led me to believe. It was a combination job."

"Pretty much. But still, you and Leonard, you were worth a lot. You can take some pride in that."

"Oh, goodie. But now Devil Red is after you."

"The guy that would pay them, he's not around anymore."

"Then why bother with me and Leonard?"

"That's personal. You may have already been on their list, and with you talkin' to Jimson, and him talkin' to them, that sealed it. You know, he was quite a talker. I think I made him nervous. He told me all about you and wantin' to know about Devil Red. The whole nine yards . . . You know why I didn't take the job to kill Devil Red?"

"Because you shot the guy who was going to pay you," I said.

She wrinkled her brows. "Well, yeah. There's that. But also there was this: I didn't want to kill Devil Red, because I know them."

"Them?"

"You've met them. Mr. Kincaid and his former wife, Ms. Clinton."

61

I couldn't have been more surprised if I had just discovered Jesus had sent me a Christmas present of the Holy Ghost with a personal note signed "Love and kisses."

"The old man and his ex-wife?" I said. "They're Devil Red?"

"Isn't that a kick?"

"Can't be."

"Can and is. Where do you think I learned my craft?"

"Them?"

"Oh, Hap, you are so cute when your jaw is on the floor. Yes. Them. Let me tell you something. Mr. Kincaid, he looks like hell, but actually, he's quite spry and doesn't need the chair or oxygen. Sometimes, garbed up like that, he uses it to get close to people. Who expects an old-looking man in a wheelchair breathing through a tube to be a killer?"

"You're foolin' with me, aren't you?"

"I'd like to fool with you, but no."

"And my client's son? His girlfriend's mother and stepfather. You know anything about that?"

She held up her hand and spread her thumb and forefinger. "Teeny bit," she said. "Mr. Kincaid and Ms. Clinton have a kind of get them all and poison the well attitude. My guess is Mini's stepfather—"

"Bert."

"Whatever. He made a wild guess they were involved, stirred them up, like you did, and they took him out. The mother, she was probably an accident. They tried to kill Leonard. You're next. I wouldn't be surprised if they went after your employer."

"Marvin?"

She nodded. "Maybe your redhead. Anyone associated with you."

"Did Jimson know Kincaid and Clinton were Devil Red?"

"He didn't really know who I was. Just my reputation. But he knew how to contact the ones you're calling Devil Red. And he did. And he contacted me. But did he know Mr. Kincaid and Ms. Clinton were in fact Devil Red? . . . No."

"You said Kincaid and Clinton trained you? There's people who do that? That's not exactly a college course."

Vanilla shifted her long legs seductively and leaned forward a little.

"Some people find the job naturally. Others have it thrust upon them. I had it thrust upon me and took to it naturally. I developed my own style, my own way. But they were my mentors. I am who I am, and I have come to embrace it. I'm almost the best there is."

"Almost?"

"There are my instructors."

I knew how good Vanilla was, and that made me realize even more what I was up against. I said, "Why would anyone want to raise you to kill?"

"Family business. Though I doubt you could call us a real family. There was never what you would call love, whatever that is. But there was affection of a sort, like you might have for a goldfish, I suppose. I don't know. Never had a pet. There was also another reason. They were a kind of factory. I wasn't the only well-trained and well-oiled cog in their machine. There were others."

"Jesus," I said.

"He didn't train there," Vanilla said. "Once we knew the trade, they hired us out. Male and female. Prostitutes of Death they called us. We got a cut of the kill, and they got the bulk. I didn't know it was unfair for a few years, us making so little. I was fifteen when I made my first hit. I wasn't even scared."

"It didn't bother you?"

"I didn't know the man I killed, so no. I'm not sure it would have bothered me if I had known him. Hell, Hap. He could have been my father. He was the right age. I don't even know why they wanted him killed. It didn't matter to me."

I let that soak in. I said, "Kincaid had a second wife, right? What did she think about all this?"

"She was unaware of the business. An airhead. She bore him two children. Ms. Clinton couldn't have children. There was an arrangement. He cared for his wife, but Mr. Kincaid really cared for Ms. Clinton. Maybe it was love. I don't know. I'm a little confused on that issue, Hap. They never really stopped being together. There was a house in town for the wife, and an estate in the country where he and Ms. Clinton spent their time. Where I was trained."

"You call them Mr. and Ms.?"

"That's how I was taught. I can't think of them any other way. But this isn't about me. This is about you, Hap. You and Leonard. Though they may have already punched his ticket. They'll wait and see. Why take an extra chance? It's my bet he never even saw his shooter. They're too good for that. But if he doesn't die, they'll be back to finish the job. And there's you."

"They leave a devil's head at the scene of their murders, staged events. Why? Why leave any indication?"

"Did Picasso sign his work?"

"They see it as an art?" I asked.

"You could say that. So do I. But I don't sign my work. They don't if time and situation doesn't permit. But they are proud of their craft. After years of doing something well, on some level, they want to be recognized, not caught. It was also a way they could challenge anyone trying to discover them. Here's our calling card. Respond if you can."

"So you deserted them at some point."

"Most do. It's the way of the job. They always have a few who live on the grounds. People who protect the place and them. They saw us as their retirement. But they haven't quit. They won't retire."

"No one should be raised to be a killer," I said.

"You could say I was exploited. But it has given me a livelihood. And I am an artist."

"You're a killer, Vanilla. That's all."

"For me it beats being a teacher or a nurse. No offense to your redhead."

"Plenty taken."

I thought I saw her blink when I said that, but it could have been the light.

"And you?" she said. "What exactly are you?"

"I suppose I'm the same as you."

She looked at me for a long moment. Her face seemed so soft, her lips so kissable. She was mesmerizing. I sat farther back from her.

"You're not like me at all, Hap. You're not even close. For me, there's no passion in the act. It is what it is, and I do it artistically. That's what makes me second to them. They are still passionate about their work. And you, you're no artist and you don't do it for money. You have reasons, views. I don't get that."

"And you're telling me all this because . . . ?"

"I don't know really. I feel we have a connection. Do you feel it?"

"I do."

"What is it exactly?"

I shook my head. "I don't know. I'm old enough to be your father."

"Maybe that's it," she said.

"I hope not. All I know is, I have to get them. They shot my friend."

"He means that much to you?" she said, turning her head slightly, as if trying to position herself to believe that idea.

"He does."

"They'll kill you."

"Maybe."

"They're better than you," she said. "I'm better than you."

"The chips aren't down yet," I said.

Vanilla shook her head slowly. "No. It won't work out for you."

"Just tell me where to find them and when."

"I don't know when, and I won't tell you where."

"You think I can't find out where they live? If I can't do it myself, I have friends who can. I'll find them. I'm asking you to speed up matters."

"I'm not one to betray."

"They betrayed you," I said. "They took a child and made a killer. You may not think that matters now, but maybe some part of you knows that isn't the life you had to have. It can't be that good a life."

I watched her face. It revealed nothing.

"It was you who got snookered, baby," I said. "The fact you came to me means you feel something other than professionalism. And if you think you're helping me by not telling me where they are, all you're doing is giving me a reprieve. They'll get to me eventually. At some point, it'll be me and them."

"Run."

"I'm not into running."

"Man's got to do what a man's go to do, huh?" Vanilla said.

"Something like that. If you're not going to help me, then leave and let me get about my business. And thanks for the warning."

Vanilla set the diet soda can on the coffee table, careful to make it fit into one of Brett's coasters. "Do you have weapons?" she asked.

"Yes."

"They certainly do. And they probably have at least two body-guards on the grounds. Maybe more. And dogs."

"Dogs."

She nodded. "Yep. And a security camera."

"Oh, good. And do the Mummy and the Wolf Man work for them too?"

"There you're safe."

"That's a relief."

"And consider this. They may or may not be home. If they were here earlier, it would take them almost two hours to go back to the estate. It's on this side of Houston. In the woods. A hundred acres or so. They would be there by now if they went home. But you don't know. It's a gamble."

"What isn't," I said. "You gonna help me, or not?"

"Get a pen and paper," she said, "and I'll draw you a map. But when I do, it's like me signing your death warrant."

62

Not long after that cheery little comment from Vanilla, I had warm clothes on, including a wool cap, the heater turned up, and my foot heavy on the gas pedal. I had a thermos of coffee and a tuna fish sandwich in a plastic bag on the seat beside me. Brett's revolver was holstered on my hip. In the glove box was my .38 Super. In the trunk, the twelve-gauge pump and ammunition for all three weapons. Also there was a toolbox with a pair of snips in it and some other things I needed. I had my clasp knife in my pocket and a roll of breath mints so as not to offend anyone I might want to stab or shoot. Marvin's sawed-off I had left at the house, replaced by my own twelve-gauge. Call me sentimental. I preferred my own gun.

Outside the air was damp with a cold mist, and the highway in the beam of the headlights looked like a ribbon of blue steel. It was late and the road was oddly empty, as if while Vanilla and I talked there had been some kind of apocalypse.

I was still trying to wrap my mind around what Vanilla had told me, and there were parts of my brain that doubted what I heard. For all I knew she was setting me up. But that didn't make a lot of sense. If she wanted me dead, she would have done it. I'd have had a bullet up my ass while I was still trying to find my house key. Not to mention that since she suspected a bomb, she could have just let it go off and they would have found my pecker in a tree the next day. And when I came downstairs from fetching my guns, she was gone, and she had taken the bombs with her.

A tidy cleanup for someone who would want me dead. And if she was using me to take out the competition, so far I wasn't proving to be that good. Neither was Leonard. A bag of crackers and cookies had got him shot, maybe killed, and Vanilla had snuck up on me while I was on my porch about to unlock a door that would have blown me apart.

I decided to believe she was on my side. I also thought maybe she had arrived at the house by means of teleportation. Where was her car? And after she had drawn the map, and I had gathered up my weapons and ammunition, how did she get out and gone so quickly, without making a sound?

That girl was creepy.

No more slacking. No more being distracted. No more feeling sorry for myself. Tonight, I had to be back on my game, like the old days.

I called Brett and asked how Leonard was doing.

"Same ole, same ole," she said. "You on the road, baby?"

"Yes."

"For reasons discussed?" she asked.

"Yes."

"That was quick."

"I had some help."

"Help?"

Brett knew about Vanilla Ride, and what she knew about her she didn't like, so I decided not to mention her.

"I'll tell you about it later," I said. "At some point I'm going to cut off my phone. Not for a while, but in the next couple of hours."

"Be careful," she said.

"Always careful," I said. "Take care of Leonard."

"You'll be back to do it."

I hesitated. "You'll take care of him, right?"

"You know it," she said.

When I finished with Brett, I called Marvin.

"I need you at the hospital. To watch Brett. To make sure she and Leonard are okay. I know I told you to sleep, but—"

"Say no more. I'm on my way."

"Marvin . . . I know what happened. I know who did it."

"Wait until you're not so steamed up, Hap. You know who it is tonight, you'll know who it is tomorrow, and you can put a plan together. Right now you're acting on anger."

"I am at that."

"Cool some."

"Now's the time," I said.

"Tomorrow we can get Jim Bob. Me. My leg is better. I'm sort of up to it now."

"No you're not."

"You're gonna hurt my feelin's, Hap."

"Right now I don't have room for that, my friend. I'm tellin' it like it is. You're not up to it, and I'm not waiting. And I don't want to pull you or Jim Bob or anyone else into this. At least not directly. This is goddamn personal. And they don't expect me to come to them. That's the only edge I got. That and knowing you're there with Brett and Leonard."

"Who are they?" Marvin asked. "Who are them?"

"I told a certain someone that if I didn't come back, they were to let you know what happened."

"Who's that certain someone?"

"You'll know if I don't come back."

It was a promise Vanilla had made me before I went upstairs to get the guns. If I didn't come back, she'd let Marvin and Brett know, warn them that Devil Red would be after them. I hoped they were smarter than me. I hoped they'd take Vanilla's advice and run. I hoped she would keep her word. I was pretty certain she would.

Marvin said, "You sound a little dramatic."

"I feel a little dramatic," I said.

I heard Marvin sigh. "You doing something like whatever the hell you're doing, and Leonard not being there . . . Man, that don't seem right. I can't think of one of you without the other. It's like Siamese twins have been halved."

"Tell me about it," I said.

63

It had started to snow. Real snow. Highly unusual for East Texas. The flakes were huge, like cotton balls. Normally snow in this area was little more than flakes that barely stuck and lasted about as long as it took to melt one on your tongue. If I hadn't been on a mission to blow people's brains out, I might have enjoyed its uniqueness and beauty. Right now, it was nothing more than a hindrance.

I wasn't far from where I wanted to go. There was a rest stop nearby and I pulled in there and tried to eat the sandwich because I thought I was crazy hungry, but it just turned out I was crazy scared. I drank a cup of coffee, slowly, because my hands were trembling. I turned on my overhead light and looked at the map Vanilla had drawn on a piece of paper. I studied it. I was close. I was very close. I turned off the light and sat and thought, and it seemed as if the trees in the roadside park were drawing nearer to me, as if the darkness between them were gathering together into something solid and demonic, trimmed in snow and ice.

I squeezed my eyes shut, and then opened them. I didn't look at the trees.

I poured another cup of coffee and tried to work my courage up as I sipped it.

My cell phone rang.

I almost jumped out of my skin.

It was Brett.

"He's slipping," she said.

"Oh, shit," I said. I felt the bit of sandwich I had eaten churn in my stomach and nearly rise up.

"Hap, I'm so sorry. They don't think he'll make it through the night."

"Goddamn it! Goddamn it to hell!"

"They let me in to see him. They said I could come in because I'm all that's here. I shouldn't have told you to go. Oh, shit, Hap. I never thought he'd die."

"He isn't dead yet."

"I held his hand. I told him you were taking care of things. I told him we loved him. Marvin is here. He's out in the waiting room."

"I told him to watch over you," I said.

"He has a gun under his coat. And he gave me one. But really, a shootout in the hospital?"

"I'm just being cautious . . . So the doctor said . . . no hope?"

"Just said he was slipping away."

"Tell Leonard I have his hat."

"What?"

"Whisper in his ear. Tell the big bastard I have his deerstalker, and if he wants it back, he'll have to take it from me. Tell him, he dies, I'll shit in it. You tell him that."

Brett laughed a little. It was strained, but it was a laugh.

"I'll tell him. If he can hear me, he'll come back just to kick your ass."

"Right now I'd let him. You go back in there, and you take Leonard's hand, and tell him his brother loves him. You hear me? You tell him that again. And you tell him what I said about his hat."

"I will," she said.

"I'm gone," I said. "And so is the phone."

I turned off the phone. I rolled down the window and tossed the coffee from the cup and threw the cup on the floorboard and sat for a moment. My stomach was really churning now. I got out of the car quickly and walked around back of it and upchucked the sandwich and the coffee. It burned my throat.

"Leonard. Don't you die," I said out loud.

I got back in the car and got a Kleenex out of the glove box and wiped my lips. I tossed out the sandwich. I put a few of the breath mints in my mouth to kill the vomit taste. I pulled away from the rest stop onto the highway.

Devil Red, I'm coming.

64

There was a little logging road, and according to Vanilla it went down behind Kincaid and Clinton's property. I took it, bumped along, almost got stuck a couple of times, made my way to where the road stopped amid what looked like the results of a nuclear strike but was in fact the end product of logging. In the moonlight, I could imagine the snow as nuclear ash, all the world dead and turned to powder.

Off to the south, that myth dissolved. The woods were thick there. Out there without lights, the moon behind cloud cover, all I could see were vague tree shapes, nature's own palisades rising thick and wild against the dark sky.

I got out with the .38 Super and my flashlight and went crunching over the frozen leaves and pine needles to the trunk of the car and opened it up, removed the shotgun, and laid it on the roof. I opened the toolbox, got the snips, and removed a little strap-on headlight like the kind you use to read in bed so as not to wake up your partner. I turned it on and slipped it over the wool cap on my head. It wasn't a big light, but it was a good enough light. I turned off the flashlight and put it in my coat pocket. I got a machete from the toolbox and the ammunition out of the trunk and stuffed my pockets with it. I made sure I had the Super's spare ammo clips where I could get to them quickly. The shotgun had a strap, so I slung it over my shoulder.

I took a pee.

I picked up a wad of snow and made a snowball in my gloved hand and threw it at a stump of a tree. I missed.

I hoped that wasn't an omen.

I was ready as I was going to be.

Way Vanilla had explained it, I had to go through the woods there, had to find my own trail, of which there were a few, and if I kept going south, I'd come to the high wall that led to the grounds of the estate. How to get over the wall was another matter, but Vanilla felt that since there were high woods on my side of the wall, on property other than their own, the logging company's property, I could maybe find access that way.

I didn't think that far ahead. If I did I'd turn around whimpering and head back to the car.

I tried several times to find a path but couldn't. The woods were thick and dead winter vines were twisted up between the trees like ancient fencing. Worse, I was no longer exactly sure which way was south. It was too damn dark, and among the trees I couldn't see anything but the whiteness of the snow and the occasional glare of moonlight on dangles of ice.

I made an attempt to follow my instincts, knowing full well that could get me in deep doo-doo, but I went ahead with it.

Hacking my way through the undergrowth, following the little beam of my head-strap light, I fought my way forward. At some point, I came upon a path through the trees and I followed that. It finally veered off to the right. I reluctantly abandoned it and started hacking again. I kept moving forward, inch by inch. I figured by the time I got through this mess and arrived, it would be two weeks from Tuesday.

Even in the cold weather, wearing all those clothes and hacking away, I was steamed and had to pause to cool it. I opened my coat and leaned against a tree. I was glad Leonard and I had been doing more workouts as of late. I had dropped a few pounds and my wind was better. Still, I was tired.

I reached up and turned off the head-strap lamp, leaned against the tree in darkness. I thought about Leonard. I thought about how long I had known him. I thought about all we had gone through. Here I was in the deep woods hacking through twisted dead winter vines and brush, and he was lying up in the hospital without me. That didn't seem right.

For a moment I considered going back, driving to the hospital to be with him. But then I thought about what Devil Red had done. I thought about how I had been sympathetic toward their killing of those who hurt their loved ones. And then I thought about what they had done to Vanilla and so many others, made them Prostitutes of Death. I was better than they were. I was much better.

I reached up and turned the light on again, and started forward.

In a very short time I saw a glow ahead of me. It was faint and blurry in the misty night. As I neared, I realized it was not a small light, but a large light that spread to my left and right, and that it was shining between the trunks of the trees. I kept going, and finally came to a thinning of the pines and saw a wall ahead of me. It was at least twenty feet high. The light was seeping over it.

Okay.

Now we separate the men from the mice.

Squeak. Squeak.

65

I walked along the edge of the barricade, feeling like a Mongol considering how to make it over the Great Wall and into China. I finally found what Vanilla suggested. A tree that grew with limbs close to the wall.

But not that close.

Kincaid and Collins kept the limbs pretty well trimmed off their side. I'd have to climb the tree and jump to the wall, and then drop down on the other side. The trick then, according to Vanilla, was to move along a certain line of trees, and then onto a long open veranda. All of this was in a blind spot for the camera. Then I had to snip a certain wire in a certain hidden place just inside the foyer, and then I had to get in, all of this without the dogs or the guards or the camera seeing me. Then I had to kill two of what she said were the greatest assassins alive, and once that was done, all that was left was to sneak out and go over the wall without being shot by the guards or having being torn apart by the dogs. Piece of cake.

I turned off my headlight, slipped the machete in a scabbard on my belt, started up the tree, which was a kind of sickly pine coated in a light casing of ice that crackled as I went. Snow drifted down on me, both from the sky and from where it had gathered on limbs. With me in my heavy coat and with the shotgun strapped on my back, I kept getting hung up, and I kept slipping on the ice, but finally I made it without falling, nestled on a limb, and gathered myself.

I was high enough up I could see over the wall. There were lights there, most of them closer to the house. There was a huge brick estate with a long veranda and a sloping roof nestled in the center of some open land. There was a line of thick-limbed trees that ran from the wall toward the house, but ended some thirty or forty feet before they got there. Everything was covered in snow.

I began to think Vanilla was way right. I was in over my head. I was having a hard enough time getting over the wall, let alone going into the house and killing Devil Red—the both of them.

Finally, I felt rested enough to scoot out to the edge of the limb, and just as I was trying to get up on it to jump, it broke, and I fell.

I lay on the ground for a long time. I had landed with the shotgun strapped to my back, so that didn't help matters either. I felt as if it had been driven into my back. The fall knocked the breath out of me and I lay there trying to get it back. I felt like the Oz Scarecrow with the stuffing pulled out. Only colder.

I was off to an excellent start, if I was a comedian.

Eventually, I felt strong enough to stand. I looked up at the tree. The limb had been my best access, and now it was gone. I went down the fence row again, this time in the direction closer to the shrubs, looking for a new way over, and finally came upon a sweet gum tree with a limb that projected just over the wall and hadn't been recently trimmed.

The problem was there were few limbs until you got up about ten feet, so I had to climb using the pressure of my palms and the soles of my shoes. The tree was damp and it was no easy business. By the time I got to the first limb I could reach, I felt on the verge of a rupture. I got hold of the limb, swung up, and sat on it for a moment. I was much closer to the line of shrubs here. I could see them through the cluttered boughs of the leaf-stripped, snow-coated tree.

I had too much stuff on me, and that was making it hard to move along, so with reluctance, I removed the machete and dropped it on the ground. I crawled out on the limb. It dipped slightly, like a horse nodding for me to get off. The wall was festooned with barbed wire and sharp pieces of metal and broken glass that had been imbedded in the cement when it was drying.

Vanilla said there was a camera, but the trees had grown large and bushy and would hide someone from sight if they came over the wall in line with them.

I was in line with them.

I eased out farther on the limb, near to its thinning tip, and that made me nervous. It was long enough that with my weight on it, it dipped over the wall. I grabbed hold of the limb and swung out, catching my pants on the glass in the wall, but only slightly. I dropped to the ground inside the compound and went down on one knee, giving things a look. The wet ice and snow came through my pants and made my knees numb.

I went at a crouch along the line of trees, and if Vanilla was right, out of camera shot. My back ached from the fall. I felt a little light-headed. Either not enough food. Too much activity. Being scared. Or a combination of all three. Fortunately, I didn't have to go number two, so I had that going for me.

66

I had only gone a few feet when I found a dead Doberman. It lay just inside the shadow of the trees, right before they broke and there was that space between them and the house.

I bent down and touched it. It was warm, and it was bloody. Bending over, I clicked on my headlight and took a look. A bullet most likely. Right through the front right chest. From the way the ground looked, the snow creased and bloody, I knew the dog had dragged itself here and died.

I clicked off the light, sat there thinking.

A thought crossed my mind. One I couldn't hold on to with

any conviction, but it was there. I decided to let it go, and to move on. I hadn't come this far to turn around and go back over the wall.

I moved to the end of the trees, stopped, and bent down and studied the gap between where I was and the veranda. As Vanilla had said, it was well lit, except right at the corner closest to me. Presumably, if what Vanilla knew about the place was the same, there wasn't an angle there that accommodated a camera. All I had to do was make a straight run into the shadows, and then, if she was right, pull myself into an indention in the wall and gather my wits, which might take a lot more time than I had available. After that, I had to move quickly, and then it was assholes, elbows, and hot ammunition.

I was about to lunge forward, and then I saw him.

He was just to the front of the veranda. A big man. A very big man. Lying on the snow-covered lawn. A rifle of some sort lay on the snow beside him. I had an idea he hadn't stopped to put his ear to the ground to hear the sweet vibrations of the earth. He was one of the bodyguards, and I was more than certain he was as dead as Abraham Lincoln; and if not, he was close enough to being dead to see Lincoln's ghost. Like with the Doberman, the snow around him was coated red.

I went across the stretch and made the edge of the veranda, and slid up against the wall. The dark indention was there, as Vanilla said. I slipped into it and caught my breath. I didn't know for a fact that the trees and that space between them to the veranda was in a camera blind, or even that I was in one now, but I had to play it that way.

I took the wire snips out of my coat pocket, and turned to where I was supposed to be able to reach through a gap and cut a wire that hooked to the camera, and another that hooked to the alarms. Snapping on my headlight, I saw there was indeed a gap, and that it was some sort of flaw in design. The concrete should have come together in that spot, but it didn't. I could get my hand in there, inside a large storage room, and flip open the little metal door that held the alarm system without any trouble, but when I flicked it open with the tip of the wire snips, the wires were already cut. I snapped off the headlight. I pulled out Brett's little revolver and moved along the veranda wall as far away from the lights as possible.

I came to the door lock Vanilla said I'd have to pick, and as I figured, the door was already cracked open.

I slipped in, held the revolver at the ready with two hands. I didn't always shoot with two hands. I had learned to shoot the Wild West way when I was a kid, and I never dropped it completely. It's not as accurate, but I can hit pretty much what I shoot at, provided it's in range and not moving too damn fast.

It was dark inside the house and I couldn't tell where I was going at first, so I just squatted down and let my eyes adjust to the shadows. I didn't turn on the little head-beam light, knowing if I did, all I was doing was giving them a little spot target on my forehead. I squatted there with my back against a wall trying not to breathe too loud. After a few minutes I could see better in the dark, make out shapes. It was all furniture as far as I could tell. Rising up, I moved across the floor with the revolver at the ready.

I stopped when a voice said, "Don't move."

67

"Jesus Christ, Vanilla," I said. "You damn near made me mess myself."

"Better than a bullet in the head," she said. "Be quiet."

She took me by the sleeve and pulled me over to a space behind a stack of boxes.

"Why?" I said.

"Now's not the time," she said. "I decided to go in with you, and right now, that's all you need to know. My take is if they have one dog outside, now dead, there might be one inside. They used to always have two. My other take is the guy in the yard isn't the only one. He was making the perimeter as I arrived. He didn't see me, but I decided it was best he go. It's best they all go."

"How many is all?" I said.

"We'll determine that as we continue. This storage room leads into a large room. The training room. That'll be our first stop. And good luck. You'll need it."

"Thanks for boosting my spirits."

"Put the pistol in your pocket, and use the shotgun. Go for heavy firepower if that's what you got."

We went out from behind the boxes and across the room, Vanilla leading the way. She moved smooth and silent as a ghost, and when we came to the double-wide doors that led into the big room beyond, we could see light through the cracks and at the bottom of it.

Vanilla spoke so that I could hardly hear her: "Ready."

"Yes," I said.

She grabbed the door handle and turned it briskly and threw the door wide. There was a guy in there, a big guy, blond-headed, handsome like a movie star. But unlike a movie star he had a real gun and it was in a shoulder holster. He was sitting at a table with a deck of cards in his hands. When the door popped back, his head snapped around, and when he saw us standing there, he turned in his chair and went for his gun, and while I was still trying to lift mine, Vanilla shot him. Her gun coughed through the silencer, like a patient in a doctor's office with a finger up his ass. The man in the chair fell back and his feet went up and a spray of blood went up with him. In that moment, a man, the dead man's card-playing partner, came out of a small room off to the side, zipping up his pants. He saw us. Vanilla shot him through the chest while he still had hold of his zipper.

She stopped by the man who had been in the chair and looked at him. He wasn't going to wake up and brush himself off. She went over to the other, and I followed after, like a puppy learning from a smarter dog. The man on the floor moaned once, opened one eye, and looked at her. She shot him through the head.

The rest of it was like a bad dream. We cruised quickly across the floor and to the double doors across the way, and Vanilla opened them without hesitation, not loudly, but not like she was still being sneaky. As she opened it, the sounds of popping hit our ears briskly. A moment later, I knew the source of the sounds.

We had stepped into it up to our necks.

It was a large long room, and there were targets at the far end, and there were four shooters taking practice on them. Three men and a woman, all young. When we stepped into the room, they turned.

And so did their guns.

I moved left and Vanilla moved right. I cut down with the shotgun and blasted the girl in her middle. She went back and down and her gun went sliding across the floor. There were two coughs to my right and two men dropped, and I let loose with the twelve-gauge again, and the last man lost his face.

"We've made enough noise," Vanilla said, "so from here on out, it has to happen fast."

There was a hallway, and it oddly split left and right. She went right without saying a word to me, walking very fast in her sensible shoes. I went left, walking less fast in one of the two pairs of shoes I owned.

I walked with the gun before me. The hallway was narrow and the walls were drab olive, or appeared that way in the near dark. There was some light from little runners near the floor. The hall went on for a long time and then it curved ever so slightly. Eventually, the hall opened up into a circular room. The room was dimly lit and there were martial arts mats on the floor. There were more mats stacked to one side, about five feet high, and across the way was an open door.

A young woman, perhaps twenty, came through the door at a rapid walk. Her long hair was tied back and looked orange in the light. She had on a bulky sweatshirt and sweatpants. She had a gun by her side. She was obviously on a mission, and that mission was me. That shotgun of mine had made so much noise I might as well have been a one-man band.

She lifted her gun with calm deliberation and fired. I was already moving, but the hair on the left side of my head fanned a little. The bullet couldn't have missed me by more than a micro fragment. It made a sound softer than Vanilla's gun; it too was silenced. I fired twice, quickly, as I dodged, the reverberation of the shotgun loud in the room.

But she was moving too. She moved like Vanilla moved. Both my shots missed, and as she fired again, I rolled, hit the matted floor, and came up behind the high stack of mats, crouching. The stuffing inside them poofed out as the silencer sneezed again.

I scurried on hands and knees farther behind the mats and put my back against the wall, about middle ways, so I could see both ends of the stack and above. The way the light overhead was set, I could see her shadow fanning around on the floor. She was climbing at a crouch over the top of the mats and was going to be above me, shooting down.

I ducked to the left of the mats, so low I was almost duckwalking, moved as quietly and quickly as possible. I glanced back at her shadow as she rose out of her crouch and was near the edge of the mats, where she expected me to be.

I stepped out from the mats in a nice noiseless move that would have impressed a mouse, lifted the shotgun just as she realized she'd been snookered and was turning to find me. I shot up and hit her in the chest. She made a noise like I had punched her and went off the mat and hit the floor with a loud thump. I couldn't see her, but I knew I had hit her good. I went around the edge of the mats and saw her lying on the floor on her back, her head propped against the wall. She still had the gun. Her face looked odd in the light. She way trying to figure who in the hell I was. Her brow was covered in sweat. Her lips were tightly clenched together. She was leaking blood all over the place. I could see where her sweatshirt had been ripped and riddled by the blast. She had her gun pointed at me. Her legs were spread out in front of her in a loose manner that made them seem as if they belonged to someone else, just borrowed for the occasion. She had a clear shot. I was about to cut down on her again, and then she lowered the gun. It lay across her lap. Her eyes were looking at me. It took me a moment before I realized she wasn't seeing anything. I didn't move for a brief moment, just stood there with my gun pointed at her. She had been an attractive kid.

"Okay," I said. "That's how it tumbles. That's how it goes."

I was startled to discover I was speaking out loud.

68

I went through the open doorway the woman had passed through and slinked along a wide corridor that was drop-dead dark at the end. I felt like I was walking into a gun barrel and someone was about to pull the trigger.

For a moment I thought about turning on my light, but figured I was outlined enough on my end without giving them a bull's-eye. I went along nervous and listening. I wasn't listening well enough, because there was movement to my right, and in that moment I realized there was an open doorway and someone was coming out of it. I turned and a shot flared the darkness, and in the flash of the gun, I saw a face.

It was Kincaid; in the brief flash of the gun he looked like a living mummy.

I swung the shotgun barrel around and caught him up along-side the head, heard his gun hit the floor and slide. But the next instant, he was twisting the barrel of the shotgun up, and it was coming out of my hands.

Moving in quick, I kicked him in the groin, and then we struggled over the shotgun. It came loose of both our hands and flew behind me and hit the wall and clattered to the floor.

Something winked in the dark and then I felt a smooth motion like the page of a book brushing across my hand, and then I felt the sting. I had been there before. A knife. I skipped backward, tried to get the pistol out of my pocket, but he was on me too fast. I made a kind of horseshoe bend as the knife passed in front of me. I felt it tug at my shirt and hit the edge of my coat as it flared wide. There was a noise as something hit the floor.

I was able to see better now, as my eyes had adjusted. I kicked the inside of his leg, and he went down on one knee. I gave him an uppercut to the chin, but he dodged it. The sonofabitch could see like an owl.

I reached in my coat pocket; it was wide open at the bottom. The knife had cut it at some point, and the damn revolver had fallen out, and that's what I had heard hitting the floor. I was scuttling backward as he came, and finally I got the clasp knife out of my pocket and snapped it open.

Seeing well enough now, I slapped a stab aside by hitting his wrist, and cut down across his forearm. Or tried to. He slapped it down and brought his knife up, and I just moved in time to keep from catching it in the throat.

He sliced again, inward, and I parried it and cut down again, this time hitting him across the arm. He let out with a hissing sound, and kicked my feet out from under me. He leaped on top of me, and I caught his knife arm and locked my legs around him. I tried to stab him, but he had hold of my wrist.

I twisted so that my blade cut him. He let go and sprang off me and tried to cut my leg, but I avoided it and he kicked up at me. I felt the knife hit my shoe.

Now we were both on our feet again. He came slashing right and left, but keeping it tight. Filipino knife work was his game, and he was good at it. Better than me. I tried to take him with a straight stab, and he disarmed me, cutting the back of my hand in the process. Weaponless, I stepped back, and my foot came down on something, and I nearly slipped.

I knew what it was. The revolver. He lunged at me. I dropped down and his thrust went where I had been. I snatched up the revolver and tossed myself on my back and fired. The shot lit up the room, but it didn't stop him. He came at me slashing. I scuttled backward. I fired again, and still he kept coming.

He leaped on me. I couldn't get a shot off. His knife made a hard thunking noise, and then he quit moving. I crawled out from under him. His knife was stuck in the floor and he was lying facedown. I turned on my head beam and kicked him over on his back.

He had taken my shots, and I saw too that I had cut him more than I thought. He may have looked like a scarecrow, but he was tough. I kicked him in the ribs a couple of times to make sure he was dead.

He didn't move. I turned to pick up the guns and the knife, and that's when he jumped on my back.

His arm went around my throat and he started choking. It was a good choke. He was shutting off the arteries. I was about to go out. I pressed in on his elbow, pressing his arm tight to my neck, just the opposite of what you might think you should do. It opened enough space on the other side, though, that the blood started to flow and I started to regain my wits. I bent down and then sprang up, and he went over my hip. When he landed, I came down on top of him, straddling his chest, and I crashed my forearm into his throat.

Once.

Twice.

Three times.

I could feel something give in his throat. He stopped struggling.

I still had my head beam on, and was still straddling him. He appeared to be a hundred years old, and at a glance skinny and weak. I knew better than that, though. He had been wiry and strong and skilled. I had been better. Or luckier.

I got up quickly and carefully. This time I wanted to be sure it was done. I found the revolver and put it in my belt, the knife in my pocket, picked up the shotgun without turning my back on Kincaid.

I went over and looked at him again.

In the light, I could see he was still breathing. He was alive still. He was a regular Rasputin.

I felt sorry for him for a moment, then I thought he was maybe the one who shot Leonard. Either him or his partner, the ex-wife.

I lifted up the shotgun and pointed it at his head, and let it go. You couldn't have told much about how he had looked after that. The hallway stank of gunfire and blood.

I moved on through the dark toward the end of the hall, the headlight on, not worrying about it anymore. Whatever came, came.

69

There were lights now, and large rooms, and I turned off the pointless headlight and went through several of the rooms until I came to a half-open door with a man on his knees, his forehead pressed to the wall.

He had fallen there. He was a large man. There was blood all down his shirt and all over the floor in a fresh wet pool. He had never known what had hit him.

There was another hallway. I went down quickly, and when I came to the end of it, there was a door slightly cracked, and there was light coming out of it. I eased over and touched the door gently, moved it aside.

Looking in, I saw Vanilla Ride squatted on her haunches, the silenced automatic in her gloved hand. Across from her, lying on the floor, her head against a couch, a hand held to her blood-gurgling throat, was Clinton. Her eyes darted toward me. She coughed and blood squirted from between her fingers. There was a little automatic lying on the floor not far from her free hand. Her fingers curled toward it, like a dying spider, but nothing more. A Doberman lay on the floor nearby. Dead, of course.

Vanilla turned her head and looked at me. She said, "You can finish her if you want. If you think it'll make you feel better."

I shook my head.

I felt empty standing there watching that woman die. Right then, it didn't matter to me what she had done. Had I come upon her first, I would have shot her myself, no doubt, but now, looking at the life ease out of her, I just felt confused.

Clinton glanced at Vanilla. She tried to say something. It sounded like "why."

"Why not?" Vanilla said. Her gun hand flicked up and the silenced weapon made a tubercular noise. Clinton's body jerked a little. A red spot appeared on her forehead, and whatever muscles were holding her head against the couch released and she rolled over on her face. The blood pooled beneath her. A pool of urine soaked out of her and its smell was rich with ammonia.

Vanilla stood. She looked at me. I can't describe what I was seeing there, but in that moment she looked much older and stranger and dangerous, a visitor from someplace far beyond Mars.

She said, "Done, and done."

70

We searched through the house, looked in all the rooms, all the nooks and crannies. There was no one left. We went out the way we had come in and stopped on the veranda in sight of the dead man in the yard. It had grown bitter cold and the snow was turning hard.

"You lied to me," I said. "You said you wouldn't get involved."

Vanilla put her gun inside her coat and looked at me. "I didn't know I was getting involved until I started drawing that map for you. Jimson, like I said, that was personal."

"I presume the map you gave me isn't really the easiest way for me to get here, is it?"

"I gave you quite a trial, didn't I?"

"You think I'd give up and go home?"

"I thought if I gave you the long and hard way here, I'd get here first, in plenty of time. Still, I didn't want you not to be a part of it. I wanted you to know it was done."

A part of me wished I had been late. From what I could see, she hadn't needed me at all.

"What made you do it?" I said.

She looked at me like that was a question that didn't immediately compute. Finally, she said, "I don't know. I learned a lot in that big room back there so long ago, the one with the mats. I learned how to fight and use a knife, ice pick, most anything I could lay my hands on. There's also a gun range farther in. Everything nice and padded and silent. There's also a bedroom that wasn't my room and it wasn't their room. You didn't see it. It's a large room, and it's silent too. I learned a lot there from Mr. Kincaid."

"I'm sorry, Vanilla."

"All part of the drill, I suppose. The males got the same."

"I'm still sorry."

"I suppose I had to close things out. I believe that's why I came, more than for you."

"How do you feel?" I said.

"Just the same."

"What now?"

"I'll show you to my car, drive you around to yours, and we go our separate ways."

"I mean what now for you?"

She shrugged and started walking across the yard. I slung the shotgun strap over my shoulder, followed, our feet crunching on the snow-covered grass. We went out through the open front gate and I swung the shotgun off my shoulder, and we got in her black Volkswagen Beetle. The one I had passed when I drove over to No Enterprise and found Jimson and his goons.

Vanilla had merely driven straight up the drive and gone inside. I don't know how she had gotten through the gate. Maybe it was open. Maybe she knew a code. After that, it had been easy. Drop the guard and the dog, and then I showed up. I'm sure she had answers to those questions, but at that point in time, I didn't really care.

As she started up the Volkswagen, I said, "I thought you were like James Bond till I saw this car. Does it have machine guns in the headlights?"

"It's maneuverable and dependable," she said. "Just like me. Did I ever tell you how maneuverable I am?"

"It's best I don't hear," I said, and she wheeled us out of there.

71

When we stopped at my car, Vanilla turned slightly in the seat, said, "You could go with me."

"You know I can't do that."

"You can."

"All right. I can. But I won't."

"The redhead?"

"That's some of it, yes."

"And Leonard."

"Yep."

Vanilla nodded. She smiled. "I don't know, Hap. I don't understand it. Why they mean so much to you."

"I don't think I can explain it."

"There's another thing I don't understand."

"What's that?" I asked.

"Why am I attracted to you?"

"It's the way I dress."

"Hardly," she said.

As I put a foot outside the door, Vanilla said, "You ever been to Europe?"

"No."

"Italy is a wonderful country," she said. "Beautiful people. The best food you can imagine. Scenery that has to be seen to be believed."

"You go there often?"

"I've never been to Italy. But I've read about it."

"You believe everything you read?"

"Only when I want to. The money I got, I don't need to do anything anymore but lie on a beach in a bikini somewhere and soak up the sun. I might just retire there. Maybe you could come see me?"

"All I can say is I owe you one," I said.

"Oh, that was a freebie. That wasn't for anybody but myself. I didn't feel good or bad about it before, but now, sitting here, I'm starting to get the warm fuzzies. I liked the way Ms. Clinton looked when I shot her. Lean over here."

I did. She kissed me gently and quickly on the lips.

"Our secret," she said.

I didn't know what to say to that.

I got out of the car with my shotgun and she backed around and was gone.

72

Vanilla should have been everything I detested in a human being, a stone killer with the conscience of a fly, but there was no denying I felt something for her. I didn't know exactly what it was. But I felt it. And she felt it back. But then again, who was I to hate someone for being a killer?

I drove back to LaBorde through a bad storm mixed with rain and snow and a vision of that young girl's face, the one I had killed in the mat room. She was just a kid. I told myself if I hadn't killed her she would have killed me. I told myself she was being trained to kill others for money. For all I knew she might have been the one who shot Leonard. There wasn't any certainty Devil Red, the two of them, or either of them had done the shooting. And if it wasn't that young woman, someday it would be, for someone.

I arrived drained and exhausted at the hospital. It was way past visiting hours, but when I got upstairs I found Brett and Marvin in the waiting room. Brett had found a blanket and was curled up in a chair asleep. Marvin sat beside her, wide awake. He nodded at me as I came in, put a finger to his lips. We went outside the waiting room to a few chairs along the wall. We sat down.

"How's Leonard?" I said.

"Better."

I sighed with relief.

"Not out of danger yet," Marvin said. "But better."

"Good," I said.

"Did you find them?" he asked.

"Yes."

"Did you take care of them?"

"Vanilla Ride took care of them mostly. I took care of some of it."

"Vanilla Ride? Our Vanilla Ride?"

"How many of them could there be?" I said.

"I'll be damned," Marvin said.

I told him all about it, everything Vanilla had told me, how it had all gone down.

He sat for a while when I finished. "So it was like Brett thought, Devil Red killed all those people for revenge. Twilla too?"

"Maybe. And then Leonard and I fell into their line of fire."

Marvin considered for a moment. "They most likely arranged the hit on Godzilla in prison, don't you think?"

"It's possible," I said. "They decided to kill us all, symbolically salt the earth. They couldn't get rid of their grief any other way. And I doubt that did it."

"What amazes me is to think they actually cared that much for their children, considering what they were, what they did to Vanilla," Marvin said.

"I think for them it wasn't child molestation or abuse in the way we think of it. I mean it comes down to the same thing, but I think for them it was just business. They were sharpening the tools of their business by making them willing and moldable. When Kincaid was away from there he was an accountant, a husband to his airhead wife, and a father to his children, who he loved. One life had nothing to do with the other."

"That's what you call compartmentalization," Marvin said.

"Yeah, I suppose it is."

"How do you feel?" he asked.

"My hand won't quit shaking. I got a few minor wounds, but that's what surprises me the most. In all the gunfire and knifing, I didn't get a serious wound. Worst thing I got was back pain from falling out of a tree. Thing I'm wondering is how we tell Mrs. Christopher that the job is done without telling her how it was done, and without getting our dicks in a crack."

"That's my job," Marvin said. "I'll find a way to satisfy her without telling her everything. There's some things she doesn't need to know. Do you think you'll see Vanilla again?"

"I don't want to. She makes me nervous."

At that moment, Brett came out of the waiting room and came over to me and grabbed me before I could stand and hugged me. I kissed her near her ear. She was crying. She fell into my lap.

"My God, I thought that was you I heard talking," she said.

She kissed me several times. I wiped away her tears. I hugged her tight. I looked at Marvin, said, "You should go home, friend."

"Yeah," he said. "I should. Call me if there's any news."

He stood and clapped his hand on my shoulder. I reached up and touched it. "Thanks."

"Don't mention it."

We went back in the waiting room, and I told her all I had told Marvin.

"I don't know how I feel about Vanilla Ride," Brett said. "You're my man."

"You know it," I said.

"Really now," Brett said. "How pretty is she?"

"She's all right."

"Hap."

"Okay. She's real pretty."

"Hap."

"All right, goddamn it," I said. "She's stunningly beautiful."

"Okay," she said, "that's enough."

73

The next morning we got word that Leonard was out of the woods, and though not ready to see visitors, much better. We decided to go home and have breakfast and get some sleep.

About noon we woke up and made love, and when we were finished, we were ravenous. We ate a quick lunch and went to the hospital. We found Rogers, Leonard's surgeon. He took us into the waiting room, where we were the only ones present. He said, "I can't figure Mr. Pine. He not only should have died in that parking lot, he shouldn't be awake and feeling as well as he is. He's not going to jump up and run a marathon or anything, but he's doing miraculously well."

"Can we see him?" Brett asked.

"Shortly," Rogers said.

About an hour later we were allowed into ICU to see him. I had hoped to have his deerstalker to wear, just to pick at him, but I didn't. I guess the cops had it.

We sat in chairs on opposite sides of the bed. We each held one of his hands. He looked rough, but he had his color back, and that wicked look in his eyes.

"So, you're gonna shit in my hat," he said, looking at me.

"You actually heard that?" Brett said.

"Yeah," Leonard said. "I wanted to answer, but couldn't. I was a little under the weather."

"I'll say," I said.

"You know," Leonard said, "bullets hurt."

"Yeah. Well, you know our motto."

"If the dick's intact, we're all right."

"That's the one"

"You're sitting funny, Hap."

"I fell out of a tree."

"Ha," Leonard said, and then licked his dry lips. "Did anyone call John?"

I felt a little ashamed. "No," I said.

"Good. I don't want him to see me like this. I don't want any goddamn sympathy from him. He comes back, I want him to come back because of the right reasons. Not because I got myself shot."

"Your surgeon said it was small caliber, and your muscle tone had a lot to do with your survival," I said. "You know what really surprises me, though?"

"What?"

"That you have any muscle tone."

"Ha, ha," he said. Then: "Brett, could you see if they would let me have a bit of soda pop? I'm craving a little something wet and sweet."

"I can ask," she said.

"Tell them I'll try not to let it squirt out the holes in my chest."

Brett got up and went away.

Leonard squeezed my hand really tight. He said, "Do you know who shot me?"

I told him who as quickly as I could. I told him what had happened to them.

"Man," Leonard said, "Vanilla is so cold and mean—"

"—her mean has to wear a hat and tie," we said together.

Leonard laughed, and then winced. "Oh," he said. "I think I shit myself a little."

"What nurses are for," I said. "Ask Brett to tell you how much she loves that part."

He grinned at me, then gradually turned serious. "How do you feel, man?"

"It got done, and Vanilla got whatever it was she needed out of it. I figure eventually we'll read about it in the papers. Someone will find them in time. They won't show to work, and then they'll go out there and find all those bodies. I don't know what the law will think."

"As long as they don't think about you, it'll be okay," Leonard said.

"I think Vanilla and I did it pretty clean. I'm even going to get rid of the shoes and clothes I had on last night. I'm leaving nothing to chance, no footprints, no clothes fibers. And since I didn't write my name in blood or draw a drawing of a devil head, I think I'll be all right."

"Of course you will," Leonard said.

"I'm going to get rid of the guns tomorrow. Except my automatic. I didn't use it. It's still clean."

"Hate to see them go," he said.

"Best bet, though. I know a good place to ditch them."

Leonard nodded.

"Vanilla, what she did," he said, "she didn't do it for me. It was for you."

"And herself."

"What I can't figure is how you got someone like Brett, and then someone looks like Vanilla, to be attracted to you. As a queer, I got to say, I don't find you attractive at all."

"Feeling's mutual," I said. "Minus the queer part."

"But, you know what?"

"What," I said.

"I love you, brother," he said, without looking right at me. "And you're the reason I came back from the dead. That, and the fact it's cold over there. And dark."

"Still," I said, squeezing his hand, "I'm not giving you that damn hat back."

BAD CHILI

Hap Collins has just returned home from working on an offshore oil rig. With a new perspective on life, Hap wants to change the way he's living, and shoot the straight and narrow. That is, until the man who stole Leonard Pine's boyfriend turns up headless in a ditch and Leonard gets fingered for the murder. Hap vows to clear Leonard's name, but things only get more complicated when another body turns up—this time it's Leonard's ex. To the police it's just a matter of gay-biker infighting, but to Hap and Leonard murder is always serious business, and these hit a little too close to home.

Crime Fiction

RUMBLE TUMBLE

Hap Collins and Leonard Pine are in for an action-packed adventure when they cross paths with a towering Pentecostal preacher, a midget with a giant attitude, and a gang of bikers turned soldiers of fortune. Even though a midlife crisis just crashed into Hap Collins like a runaway pickup, he's still got his job, he knows his best friend, Leonard Pine, will always be there for him, and, of course, he's got his main squeeze, Brett Sawyer. Things hit a new low, however, when Brett's daughter, Tillie, who's been walking on the wrong side of the law suddenly stands in need of a rescue. It won't be easy—it never is—but nothing is going to stop Hap and Leonard as they hit the road destined for Hootie Hoot, Oklahoma, to shake things up.

Crime Fiction

CAPTAINS OUTRAGEOUS

Hap Collins and Leonard Pine find mucho trouble, this time in Mexico, when they come face to face with a nudist mobster, his seven-foot strong-arm, an octogenarian knife-touting fisherman, and, somehow, an armadillo. When Hap Collins saves the life of his employer's daughter, he is rewarded with a Caribbean cruise, and he convinces his best friend, Leonard Pine, to come along. However, when the cruise sails on without them, stranding them in Playa del Carmen with nothing but their misfortune and Leonard's ridiculous new hat, the two quickly find themselves drawn into a vicious web of sordid violence.

Crime Fiction

VANILLA RIDE

Hap Collins and Leonard Pine, the kings of East Texas mischief and mayhem, return in this full-throttle thriller to face off with the Dixie Mafia. When Leonard is asked to rescue a teenage girl from a lowly drug dealer, he gladly agrees and invites Hap along for the ride. Everything goes according to plan, until they find out the dealer is a member of the Dixie Mafia. A wild gun fight ensues, after which Hap and Leonard are arrested. Turns out, however, that the law needs a favor and if Hap and Leonard can do the deed they'll be free to roam. There's one problem, the Dixie Mafia's new hired gun— the legendary assassin Vanilla Ride. Filled with breakneck action, gut-busting laughs, and one gigantic alligator, this hilarious novel is as hot as a habanero pepper.

Crime Fiction

THE BOTTOMS

A thriller with echoes of William Faulkner and Harper Lee, *The Bottoms* is classic American storytelling in its truest, darkest, and mort affecting form. It's 1933 in East Texas and the Depression lingers in the air like a slow-moving storm. When a young Harry Collins and his little sister stumble across the body of a black woman who has been mutilated and left to die in the bottoms of the Sabine River, their small town is instantly charged with tension. When a second body turns up, this time of a white woman, there is little Harry can do to stop his Klan neighbors from lynching an innocent black man. Together with his younger sister, Harry sets out to discover who the real killer is, and to do so they will search for a truth that resides far deeper than any river or skin color.

Fiction

LEATHER MAIDEN

After a harrowing stint in the Iraq war, Cason Statler returns home to the small East Texas town of Camp Rapture, where he drinks too much, stalks his ex-wife, and takes a job at the local paper. There he uncovers notes on a cold case murder. With nothing left to live for and his own brother connected to the victim, he makes it his mission to solve the crime. Soon he is drawn into a murderous web of blackmail and deceit. To make matters worse, his deranged buddy Booger comes to town to lend a helping hand.

Fiction

LOST ECHOES

Since a mysterious childhood illness, Harry Wilkes has experienced horrific visions. Gruesome scenes emerge to replay before his eyes. Triggered by simple sounds, these visions occur anywhere a tragic event has happened. Now in college, Harry feels haunted and turns to alcohol to dull his visionary senses. One night, he sees a fellow drunk easily best three muggers. In this man, Harry finds not only a friend that will help him kick the booze, but also a sensei who will teach him to master his unusual gift. Soon Harry's childhood crush, Kayla, comes and asks for help solving her father's murder. Unsure of how it will affect him, Harry finds the strength to confront the dark secrets of the past, only to unveil the horrors of the present.

Fiction

SUNSET AND SAWDUST

In the middle of a cyclone, beautiful, red-haired Sunset Jones shoots her husband, Pete, dead when he tries to beat and rape her. To Camp Rapture's general consternation, Sunset's mother-in-law arranges for her to take over from Pete as town constable. As if that weren't hard enough to swallow in Depression-era East Texas, Sunset actually takes the job seriously, and her investigation into a brutal double murder pulls her into a maelstrom of greed, corruption, and unspeakable malice. It is a case that will require a well of inner strength she never knew she had. Spirited and electrifying, *Sunset and Sawdust* is a mystery and a tale like nothing you've read before.

Fiction

VINTAGE CRIME/BLACK LIZARD
Available wherever books are sold.
www.randomhouse.com
www.weeklylizard.com

Printed in the United States
by Baker & Taylor Publisher Services